To special friends, special times (including menopause) Thanks for your help, support and love.

& Juli and

RITES OF PASSAGE

A Novel

Luckii Ludwig

Published by ForeReel Publications
Davis, California

For my sister, Yram

CHAPTER ONE

The envelope read, *"Marge Sinclair, Sinclair Construction, PO Box 798, Minot, ND 58587"*. The letters were gold-embossed, slightly raised, and beautifully scripted.

Marge almost passed over the envelope as she sorted through the afternoon mail. "Probably another damn invitation to something I don't want to attend," she muttered.

Her eye caught the return address—*Rites of Passage Castle, PO Box 50, Lake Tahoe, NV 89895.*

She turned over the envelope with her gnarled hand and its bright-red nails and held it up to the light. "What the hell?" she thought.

Marge unbuttoned the top button of her gray and blue flannel shirt, exposing a bit of cleavage. She kicked off her aging, worn, brown cowboy boots and flopped into a chair.

She looked around to see if Walter was still inside, but he wasn't. After brushing her stringy blonde bangs off her forehead and shoving the rest of the mail aside, she fumbled with the flap with short, slender fingers.

"Might as well take a look," she mused.

One corner of her mouth turned upward in a half smile as an elegant, gold-embossed invitation slid out. Her blue eyes opened wide. Before she could catch her breath, a frown formed on her brow as she read.

*You are cordially invited to attend
the first Rites of Passage Conference
for women turning fifty. It consists of
three days and two nights, all expenses
paid, at the beautiful Rites of Passage
Castle on Lake Tahoe.*

*The goal of the conference is to
establish a Rite of Passage for all
future women turning fifty.
The conference dates are
June 2-4, 1995
RSVP by April 1, 1995, for
accommodation selection.
1-(800)-555-9550*

Marge turned the card over, but the back was blank. "What the hell is this, a joke? What's a rite of passage?"

She glanced at the calendar. It was the end of February. Her eyes moved slowly toward the window. It was a typical North Dakota day, cold and windy, but at least it wasn't snowing. She had her fill of the record snowfall that year, and she looked forward to spring. That meant more work for her construction company.

Things were slow that winter. No one was building or remodeling. The winter had been the worst she could remember with all the snow. Many parts of the state still felt the effects of the recent recession.

"Oh, sure," Marge thought. "June is when things will be busiest for me, and someone I don't know wants me to take a vacation. I'm supposed to drop everything for three days and head for Lake

Tahoe to help a bunch of old women have a passage into something? Fat chance."

Although she finally convinced herself it was a sales gimmick or a joke, she slipped the card into the pocket of her down jacket instead of throwing it away.

"I'll show it to Greg. He'll get a kick out of it." She laughed, then stood and tightened the brown leather belt holding up her skintight Levi's and continued sorting the mail. The bills went into a box labeled, *To Be Paid.*

She was almost finished when Walter came in. He removed his wide-brimmed hat and shivered from the cold.

"Hi, Honey. Anything good in the mail?" he asked.

Marge didn't look up. "Nothing important, just a few bills we can't pay, anyway."

"Oh, good. No bad news. I'll take a shower and try to warm up. I got that fence fixed."

"Good for you," she said coolly. "I have to go into town for a few things. I'll be back later."

Walter looked dejected. "Will you be back in time for dinner?"

"I don't think so. There are several people I need to see, and I have a couple of leads for work I need to follow up. I'll grab a quick bite in town, but I won't be too late."

He lowered his head and left the room without a word. Marge felt guilty, but not enough to stay home. There weren't any leads— she would have dinner with Greg.

"Why should I feel guilty?" she wondered. "It's not as if Walter and I have much of a marriage left. We don't sleep together, and I'm sure he's seeing someone else, too."

She got her coat and went out to her old 1979 brown Jeep. She loved it. It was with her longer than anyone else. The hubcaps had been missing for a long time, but she didn't care. That just made it

7

easier to change a flat. The heater didn't work as well as it once did, but that didn't bother her. The driver's window was cracked and let cold air flow on her.

The drive to Minot only took twenty minutes. The roads were clear, but they could be treacherous during the winter. She and Greg had to change their plans more than once, because she was snowbound at home with Walter. She looked forward to her evening with Greg.

When she drove up, Greg bounded out the front door in his favorite raveled gray sweatshirt and Levi's with holes in the knees and under his left buttock, where Marge usually placed her hand. He was barefoot, which made her grimace.

"Hi, Sugar," he greeted. "I thought you'd never get here."

"Jesus, Greg. I said I'd be here by four, and it's a quarter to."

Greg was twelve years younger than Marge, and she resented him occasionally for having so much more energy. He opened her door and hugged her.

"I know it's not four yet, but it seems like forever since I last saw you, and I couldn't wait. I got all excited." He kissed her face and began working his way to the back of her neck.

"Greg, please! The neighbors!"

He waved his hand. "Forget them. I already told most of them about us and how you'll divorce your husband to marry me." He grinned.

"Oh, Greg, quit joking."

"I'm not. You think people don't know about us? The whole town's talking about it. I'm sure even Walter knows by now. Besides, you are going to marry me, aren't you?"

She got out of the jeep. "I didn't come here to talk about marriage. I came to have dinner with you and get laid."

His smile widened, and his brown eyes danced. "That's what I love about you, Marge. You're sentimental and unsure of what you want. Come in. I've got dinner ready."

"You cooked?" She was amazed.

"Yeah, me and the Golden Palace. I figured the faster we had dinner, the faster we could hit the sack. I didn't think you'd spend the night with me, so I didn't want to waste any time."

Marge hesitated. "You know I'd love to spend the night, but I...."

"I know. You're afraid Walter will find out. I'm sure he already knows. He has to be told sometime. We need to talk about that."

Marge walked into the house without answering, then went straight to the refrigerator.

"Help yourself to a beer, Baby," Greg called from the other room. "I stocked up on Michelob for you."

She reached for a cold beer, twisted off the cap, and tossed it into the wastepaper basket. She missed, but left the cap on the floor where it fell, and walked into the living room.

"Where are you?" she called.

"In the dining room."

"I didn't know you had one." She followed the sound of his voice.

He was grinning when she found him. "Actually, I don't have one, but I turned this part of the room into one for a romantic dinner with candles."

Marge looked at the table. She was almost afraid to ask what was under the tablecloth because she never knew Greg to have a real table in the house. He must have put some boxes together. The table held candles and a large bouquet of flowers.

"Where the hell did you find fresh flowers this time of year?" she asked.

"Fooled you!" He danced in circles. "Feel them. They're fake, made of silk or something, but they sure look real. Like them?"

"Yeah, sure, I guess. What's the occasion?"

Greg was coy. "You'll find out. Sit." He held a chair for her. "I ordered your favorite Chinese food—sweet and sour spareribs, chicken fried rice, egg foo yong, and the special beef chow mein."

"Greg, this is really nice. I'm starved, too. What are you going to eat?"

He laughed, "I can get more if we need it."

Marge ate twice as much as he did. He was too excited to eat. After he finished, he bounced out of his chair.

"Don't worry about the dishes," he said. "I put clean sheets on the bed, and we can move the candles into the bedroom."

"Christ, Greg. Not so fast. I'm not done eating. I'll need a cigarette before we hit the hay. What are you so wound up about?"

He straddled his chair. "Sorry. I'm a little hyper tonight. It's just that I bought you a present, and I've been dying to give it to you. I was going to wait until after we made love, but, as long as we're sitting here, I might as well give it to you now."

"A present? For me? Greg, you shouldn't have. That's so nice and everything, but...."

"No buts. Here. Open it." He handed her a small box.

It looked like a ring box, but Marge was certain he wouldn't buy her a ring. It could be another piece of jewelry, but she didn't wear any other kind. She slowly worked the ribbon loose and looked at Greg, who was squirming with impatience.

She opened the box and found a large sapphire ring. Her mouth fell open as she stared at it.

"Do you like it?"

"Greg, it's beautiful, but I don't understand."

"It's like an engagement ring. I knew you didn't like diamonds, so I thought something that went with your eyes would be neat."

"An...engagement ring?" she stammered. "Greg, I'm still married. We can't be engaged. I...."

"Don't say anything now, just take the ring and think about it. You aren't in love with Walter anymore, and the two of you certainly don't have a marriage. I want you to know how much I love you and want to marry you. Just think about getting a divorce. Then, you can wear the ring and we'll be engaged. We can get married whenever you want."

"Greg, this is so sweet. The ring's gorgeous, but I can't keep it. I don't wear that many rings. I don't even know if I'm in love with you. I'm not sure how I feel about anything. Christ, I'm turning fifty this year. I'm having hot flashes and crazy mood swings."

He leaned across the table and took her hand. "Don't say anything now."

"I'll have to leave this here. I can't take it home."

He stood, still holding her hand. "Come on. Let's go to bed. We'll talk later."

For the first time since she met Greg, she wasn't in the mood for sex. She was so upset by his proposal, she couldn't even fake an orgasm. She hadn't planned on marrying him. All she wanted was a good time.

After Greg finished, Marge lay in bed and smoked a cigarette. He was so excited about the evening, he hadn't noticed she wasn't in tune with him that night.

Then she remembered the invitation she received earlier. "Greg, I almost forgot. I got something in the mail today. It's the strangest thing. I want to show it to you and see what you think."

"Great. Where is it?"

She slid out of bed and into Greg's tattered white terry cloth robe. "Be right back. It's in my jacket." She sauntered out of the room, letting the robe fall open to expose her breasts. She stopped in the kitchen to grab a beer, and then retrieved the invitation.

When he read it Greg said, "This could be great. We could go to this castle together and have an early honeymoon."

"That's not what this is all about. It has something to do with women and rites of passages."

"What's that?"

"How the hell should I know? It's some kind of women's thing, like when she goes through menopause or something."

"Why don't you call and find out? It's an 800 number. Call from here. Go ahead. Maybe both of us can go."

Marge reached for the phone, dialed and waited while the telephone rang. A voice answered promptly.

"Rites of Passage Castle. How may I help you?"

"Hi. This is Marge Sinclair. I received an invitation in the main today, and I was wondering...."

"Marge! How good of you to call so quickly. I'm Julia."

"Well, listen, Julia, I'm only calling for more information. I'm not sure I want to participate. I have no idea what this is about."

Julia laughed. "I'm certain of that. This is something new we're doing, and we hope you'll be part of our first-ever Rites of Passage Conference."

"What do you do at this conference?"

"We're going to develop a rite of passage that women turning fifty can go through to achieve the recognition and respect they deserve."

"And, you think I can help?"

"We're positive of it."

"Is this some kind of sales gimmick to make me buy something?"

"Not at all."

"How'd you get my name?"

"Through an extensive computer search."

"What were you looking for?"

"Women who would turn fifty this year. That's all."

"What do I have to do?"

"Just say you'll come. You won't regret it, I promise. Everything will be taken care of, and you'll return home a new woman."

Marge snickered. "Sounds like a good idea. Okay, I'll come. Can I bring a guest?"

"No. This is just for you, but you won't be disappointed. Before you hang up, you do have your choice of accommodations. We have penthouse suites, motor homes, bungalow cabins and tents for camping. Which do you prefer?"

"Not a tough decision. I want a penthouse."

"Very well. You'll receive more information in the future. Air travel arrangements will be made for you."

"There aren't many airplanes that fly into Minot."

"Don't worry about that, Dear. We'll send a private jet for you. You'll receive the details later. Thanks again for accepting our invitation."

"Sure. My pleasure, I think." Marge stared at the receiver before hanging up.

CHAPTER TWO

When Marge went home, she wasn't sure what to tell Walter. She knew she had to deal with the issue of Greg sooner or later, but she was willing to settle for later.

She also didn't know what to say about her trip to Lake Tahoe. She hardly knew what to think herself, except that for some reason, she knew she had to go. Besides, she wasn't into sharing things with Walter anymore. The drive home was short, and she didn't have much time to think.

Walter was sitting at the kitchen table when she came in.

"How'd everything go?"

"What? Oh, yeah. Fine, I guess."

He stood. "Get the job?"

"Job?"

"The job you said you went to town about."

"I don't know. I don't think so."

"Marge, why don't we talk? I know things aren't going well between us right now, but maybe if we hashed things out, we could resolve something."

"Maybe, but, to be honest, I'm tired. I don't know what to say, and I've got a lot on my mind." She walked past him to get a beer from the refrigerator.

"Like what? You never talk to me anymore. You never have time for words, or you're too tired. I have no idea what's going on except what I hear from other people."

Marge gasped. "Such as?"

"You know, the same old thing, that you're shacking up with another guy."

"People are saying that?" She was flabbergasted.

His voice went up. "Jesus, Marge! Do you think I'm stupid and blind? Do you think I need people to tell me what you're up to? I've known you a long time. You won't go this long without a man in your bed, and it sure as hell hasn't been me. Everyone's talking about it. I hoped it would blow over, but that isn't happening."

"Walter, please, can't we talk about this later? It's been a long day."

"Long day, hell!" he shouted. "Because you've been screwing your brains out? You haven't done a damn thing other than that and drinking beer. Oh, excuse me." He bowed sarcastically. "You brought in the mail."

"The mail," she thought. "Maybe I can change the subject."

"Here." She shoved the invitation in his face. "Take a look at this. This is one thing I've been dealing with."

He read the invitation and envelope, then laughed. "What the hell is this, a tryst you dreamed up with your boyfriend? I won't fall for that."

"Jesus, Walter. I don't know what it's about either. I called them, and they said it was an all-expense-paid conference for women only."

He was furious. "You think I'll believe that shit? I may've closed my eyes to a lot of things, but not this time."

"There's a toll-free number, Walter. Call it yourself and act like a fool. I'm going to bed. We'll discuss it in the morning."

She finished her beer, slammed the empty on the countertop, and stormed out of the room.

She didn't sleep well that night, and she wasn't certain if Walter even came to bed. When she woke, she was alone. As she came downstairs, she smelled fresh coffee. Walter sat at the kitchen table.

"Care for some coffee, Marge?"

"Yes, thank you. It smells great."

"Look, Marge, I'm sorry about last night. It's just that...."

"Don't say anymore. You're right, we need to talk."

"I called that place last night. They were snotty to me, like I had no right to call them. The lady was offended that I was checking on you. Anyway, if it's something you really want to do...."

"I don't need your permission to do this. I already accepted. I'm not sure why I'm going, but it's something I feel I need to do for myself. I'm going. Getting away from here will do me good."

"What about us?"

"What about us? There hasn't been an us for a long time."

"Maybe there could be if you weren't out screwing with your boyfriend."

"Walter, this has nothing to do with him. It's between you and me. Frankly, we haven't had anything in common long before he came along. I don't know if I'm in love with you. I care a great deal about you, but...."

"But, you're in love with what's-his-name?"

"No."

"Is it true he's younger than you?"

Marge was irritated. "Christ, Walter. Okay, he is younger than me. Big deal. This still has to do with you and me, not anyone else."

He was silent for a moment. "I still love you, but I don't understand you. You've changed a lot and grown away from me. I also think you're drinking too much. Maybe this is a mid-life crisis."

"God, don't you just love it?" She flung her arms wide.

"Whenever there's a problem between a man and a woman, it's always the woman's fault. He is never to blame. Men attribute the problem to a female condition, like having her period, PMS, or menopause. If you want to put all the blame on me, then call it what it is, menopause, not a damned mid-life crisis. Did you ever stop to think women no longer want to be dominated and controlled by men so they can stop having babies and start doing something for themselves?"

Walter didn't know what to say. He hadn't seen her adamant and spunky in years. He couldn't remember the last time she talked to him, let alone talked back. "So, what do we do?"

"I need space. I'd like you to move to the guest cottage. I want a clear mind to decide what's best for me."

"You mean not see you anymore?"

"Of course not. You can come into the house for meals and such. I just don't want you hanging over my shoulder, breathing down my neck, or sleeping beside me."

"For how long?"

"Until I get back from Tahoe."

"That's a long time."

She stared at him, threw on her jacket, and went outside for a walk. Lobo, her German Shepherd, saw her heading toward the barn and followed.

The chill morning air showed in Marge's breath when she spoke. "Oh, Lobo, a woman's best friend. If only men were more like you. Perhaps then I'd be able to get along with them. I always seem to pick the wrong man, but I never have trouble with dogs."

Lobo cocked his head to one side as Marge leaned down to hug him. He whimpered.

"I know. I don't pick men for who they are. Hell, I didn't even know Walter when we married. He was good in bed, and I thought that would translate into being good at all the other things

18

I wanted him to be, too. I should've checked his breed. We don't have the same interests. He doesn't even like dogs."

Lobo growled and stopped walking.

Marge laughed. "I didn't mean he doesn't like you. Everyone likes you. Well, to be honest, he only tolerates you. He's not a dog person. I need someone who likes having dogs in the house."

As she thought about it, Marge became painfully aware that she checked out her dogs more closely than she ever checked her men. She didn't even know Greg's last name when she first slept with him.

"Lobo, I know all about your parents, their temperament, what kind of physical problems your line has had over the years, and your life expectancy. What do I know about men? If they're sexually compatible, and I get those funny butterflies in my stomach when they touch me, that's my extent of checking them out. At that point, I figure they must be the right one."

She kept walking. "I've been a fool, Lobo. I need to take a good look at myself. I'm going to this conference at Lake Tahoe. They promised to turn me into a new woman. I hope so. I need some changes."

Lobo wagged his tail as Marge kissed his head. "Don't worry, my sweet prince. I'll never leave you. When I come back from Tahoe, I guarantee things will be different around here."

CHAPTER THREE

The envelope read, *Kathryn Chandler, Forbis, Johns and Chandler, Attorneys at Law, 2300 Mt. Vernon Blvd., New York City, NY 12105.* The letters were gold-embossed, slightly raised, and beautifully scripted.

"What's this?" She thumbed through her mail. Of all the envelopes on the desk, none caught her dark eyes except the one with the return address, *Rites of Passage Castle, PO Box 50, Lake Tahoe, NV 89895.*

Kate leaned back in her burgundy leather chair and fondled the envelope in her long, slender fingers. A smile formed in one corner of her red lips. "I never got a letter from a castle before. This should be good."

With the index finger of her left hand, she slid a long, manicured nail under the flap. The envelope popped open, and she nudged out what appeared to be an invitation.

"An invite?" Her brow wrinkled.

She read the message for the conference and slowly turned the card over to check the back. It was blank. She stood and paced the room, twisting the invitation in her hands.

"What the hell?" she asked. "This must be a joke. I don't know anyone in Lake Tahoe. I've never even been there."

She walked to her twenty-seventh floor window and looked out. A cold rain fell, and clouds hung low over the city. It didn't give her much of a view. Still, no matter how cold the rain was, she liked that better than snow. She held the invitation to the light and turned it in her hand, but no clues appeared.

"Of course it's a joke," she laughed. "Look at the RSVP date, for crying out loud. April Fool's day? Who'd try to pull a prank on me?"

She looked down at a wrinkle on her gray-striped Liz Claiborn skirt. She loved that skirt, and it went well with the dark-gray jacket and red scarf she bought the previous week.

"I've been sitting too much. Now, I'll have to send this to the cleaners before I can wear it again."

She straightened a seam in her dark stockings and wondered why she ever thought it would be chic to have seams like in the old days. One by one, as she called friends' names to mind, she dismissed them as being involved in the prank.

Her train of thought was interrupted by the buzz of the intercom. "Yes?"

"Kate? It's Bob. Can you come in here for a minute?"

"Be right there." She tossed the invitation onto the desk.

Kate walked briskly down the short hallway to Bob Forbis' office. She paused to check herself in the mirror and smiled. She liked how she looked and was glad she quit straightening her hair. Not only did her natural hairstyle look good, it was easier to take care of.

"Straightening my hair was a waste of time and money." She laughed, thinking about the first time she walked into Bob's office with her new hairdo. He didn't know what to say.

"Well...." He scrambled for words. "I guess I like it. I mean, I never saw your hair so curly. It...I don't know...it makes you look so...African American."

"But, Bob, I am African American."

"Oh."

She came a long way since the early days when he first hired her. She was certain the only reason she got the job was because of her race. Bob needed a minority in the firm, but she had proved her worth many times over until she was given a full partnership. With Bob's impending retirement, her partnership would become even more valuable.

"Hi, Bob." She closed the door behind her. "What gives?"

He motioned her to a chair. "Sit down. I've got some news you won't like."

She sat quietly, resting her heel on the leg of the overstuffed chair. "What?"

"P&G has hired a new defense counsel for your case against them."

She jumped up. "What the hell kind of stalling tactics are they trying now?"

Bob stood, too. "Actually, they claim they aren't stalling. They say they want the matter to proceed as scheduled. Don't you want to know who they picked?"

Kate was pacing. "I don't give a damn who they hire as long as we can get this show into court soon. I have an airtight case against them. The lawyer doesn't matter."

She turned and faced Bob. From the look on his aging face, she knew there was more than just a new lawyer. "Okay. I can see you're dying to tell me. Who's the new mouthpiece?"

"Ronald Miller."

She stared in shock. "You don't mean my Ronald Miller?"

"The same."

She retained her maiden name after she married Ronald, because she wanted her own career, not just to be known as an attorney's wife.

"But he's a criminal attorney. He doesn't know anything about corporate law."

"They seem to think criminal charges might evolve out of some of the charges you lodged against them."

Kate was furious. "He can't do this. It's not right. Isn't there some kind of conflict of interest involved? Do they think I'll go lighter on them, because my husband represents them? I'll kill him for getting involved in this one without having the guts to tell me."

"Have you discussed the case with him?"

"Not really. I said I was going for the jugular and tried to give him a few details, but he didn't seem interested. He knows it's my case. How the hell can he take it?"

Bob walked over to her. "Calm down. He's probably having one of his associates deal with it. I'm sure he won't personally get involved, knowing it's your case."

"That's not the point!" She was furious. "It's still his firm involved. How dare he defend one of my cases?"

Bob put his arm around her. "Listen, Kate, it's getting late. Why don't you go home and talk to him? See what you can find out. I'm sure there's a logical explanation."

"Sure. I can hardly wait to hear it. It'll be interesting to see how he tries to explain this one. I can't believe he didn't tell me." She stomped her foot.

As she headed toward the door, she stopped and turned. "You aren't thinking about any changes on this end, are you?"

"Not on your life. It's your baby. We'll win with you no matter who they pit against you."

"Thanks, Bob. See you tomorrow."

Kate thundered into her office, picked up her purse, and threw it across the room. "Damn him!" she muttered. "What's he trying to pull? He knows this is my case."

She tossed a few things into her briefcase, then, at the last minute, added the invitation when it caught her eye.

She was so upset, she almost took the wrong subway train

home. She knew Ronald wouldn't be there yet, but she was too angry to stay at the office and work. She'd been preparing the case for months. She had proof—albeit circumstantial- that P&G intentionally subjected many of its workers, most of whom were African Americans, to toxic chemicals. They were liable for millions of dollars in damages to the workers and their families. How could Ronald even think of defending such a company?

When she arrived home, she hung up her coat and briefcase, then thought better of it and took the briefcase into her office and locked it in her desk.

Ronald waltzed in several hours later. "Hi, Sweety. I brought Chinese food. Hope you're hungry."

Kate stormed into the kitchen. "What is this, a peace offering? I'm too upset to eat. What the hell are you trying to pull?"

Ronald pulled away from her. "Oh, I see you found out."

"Found out?" she shouted. "Of course I found out. Did you think I wouldn't? I can't believe you didn't have the balls to tell me yourself. What were you thinking?"

"Now, Kate. I meant to tell you. We haven't exactly had much time together lately. I never found the right time to bring it up."

"The right time? That would've been when the idea first popped into your head. You could've yelled it down the hall as I was leaving for work. This is my case. Even if it wasn't, I can't imagine you defending a company that has wronged so many people, most of them ours."

Ronald moved to the cupboard and pulled down two plates. "First, there are two sides to this story. Second, it wasn't my idea to take the case."

"Whose idea was it?"

"Actually, Jeffrey said...."

"Jeffrey? That dweeb? You let your racist partner talk you

into this?"

"He said it would be good exposure for the firm, and your proof's all circumstantial. You don't have any real proof the company did anything wrong."

Kate threw her hands into the air. "Jesus. You believed him? I certainly hope for your sake he's the one handling this. I'll fry him."

"Well...I'm handling it. Jeffrey thought it would look better for an African-American lawyer to defend them."

"You idiot! You went along with it? Let's throw some doubt on this. Obviously, if her husband defends them, there's a question of their guilt."

"Look, Kate, under the circumstances, maybe we'd better not discuss this anymore. We can't talk about the case."

"Maybe we should carry it even further, Ronald."

"What do you mean?"

"I mean I don't want to discuss anything with you, not even the weather. I sure as hell don't want to eat dinner with you. I don't want you in this house while this case is underway. I'm not going to compromise my position. Right now, I can't stand the sight of you, and I don't want you hanging around and prying into what I'm doing."

"This is my house, too. I have a right to be here. What makes you think I'd pry?"

"Anyone who takes a case against his own wife would do anything. I don't trust you anymore. It's not fair to have to face you during one of my most important cases. I don't need you breathing down my neck. Move out this weekend."

"But...."

"No buts. Get out, or get off the case. I don't want to see you again until this is over."

Kate left the kitchen and went into her office, slamming the door behind her. She paced, then sat on the sofa and tried to breathe deeply to relax. Finally, in desperation, she remembered the invitation.

She reread it. "I sure as hell can't concentrate on anything, so I might as well call. It wouldn't hurt to find out what this is all about. It can't be half as crazy as things are around here right now."

She dialed the number.

"Rites of Passage Castle. How may I help you?"

"I'm not sure. I received an invitation today, and I'm curious what it's about."

"Good of you to call so soon, Kate."

"Wait a minute. How'd you know who I am?"

The woman laughed. "Excuse me. We have one of those telephones that lets you know the incoming number. Since it was from New York, I assumed it was you."

"There are millions of people from New York. It could've been anyone."

"You're the only person in New York who got an invitation."

"How'd you get my name?"

"We did a computer search of women turning fifty this year."

Kate felt uneasy. "You found only one person in New York who will turn fifty this year?"

"Actually, we're looking for special people. Your name was selected. We check people out before we invite them to the castle. I hope you don't mind."

"Fine. Who are you?"

"Oh, how impolite of me. Allow me to introduce myself. I'm

Julia Worthington."

"You're in charge of this conference?"

"Yes, I am."

"What kind of conference is it?"

"It's something new. We've never done it before. We'd like you to be part of it. We intend to develop a rite of passage that women turning fifty can go through to achieve the recognition and respect they deserve."

"What's that got to do with me? I don't know anything about rites of passage."

"No one does. That's why we're having this get-together. Since you'll be fifty in July, we thought you might like to be part of this special event. You won't regret it. You'll come, won't you?"

"Who sponsors this?"

"It's funded through a private foundation."

"What's your background?"

"I've spent my entire life studying human behavior."

Kate hesitated, "I don't know."

"You have nothing to lose. You'll probably need a nice break after your upcoming trial."

"How do you know about that?"

"We know a lot about you from our computer search."

Kate couldn't believe such information was so readily available, but she was curious about Julia and her foundation. Besides, a break would be good after the trial.

"June, you say? Maybe I could use a break by then. Okay, I'll come. What do I have to do?"

"You won't have to do anything except pack," Julia said happily. "We'll send further information so you'll know what to bring. Everything will be taken care of. You have your choice of accom-

homes, and tents for camping."

"I always wanted to vacation in a motor home. I'll take that."
Under her breath, Kate added, "Besides, I can always drive off if
this gets too weird."

"Very good. You'll be sent information about your air travel
arrangements. A private jet will pick you up. Thanks for accepting
our invitation."

"I hope I won't regret it."

Julia chuckled. "Trust me, Kate. You won't. This will change
your life."

Kate grinned and hung up. "I could handle that," she thought.

CHAPTER FOUR

In the weeks to come, Kate found herself embattled in a mix of heavy emotions and an increasingly bitter court fight against the company Ronald defended. The newspapers played up the courtroom antics whenever they could.

Ronald moved out after the confrontation and moved in with one of the junior partners in the firm.

All Kate told Bob was, "Ronald moved out of the house."

"I'm sorry to hear that, Kate. There's no way you two can work things out?"

"We didn't try. I was so angry, I refused to listen to anything he said."

"Did he mention the case?"

"He said there were two sides to the story. I didn't give him a chance to say much else."

Bob thought for a moment. "How will this affect your handling of it?"

"Hopefully, it won't. My case was well-established long before Ronald became involved. As far as I'm concerned, he's just another lawyer. I still think we've got a strong case, and I'm more determined to win than ever."

"What about your marriage?"

"I don't know," she confessed. "I can't think about it right now. I want to resolve the case first. That's my top priority. I'll deal with my marriage, or what's left of it, afterward."

"I hope things work out for the best," Bob smiled.

Kate nodded. "Thanks. Me, too. By the way, I'm taking a few days off the first week in June for a short vacation, even if this isn't over."

"June? That's a long way off. Going anywhere special?"

"As a matter of fact, yes. I'm going to Lake Tahoe the second through the fourth."

"Tahoe? In California? Ever been there?"

Kate stifled a giggle. "No, I haven't. I think we'll be on the Nevada side."

"Think?"

"You'll probably find this a little strange, but I've been invited to an all-expenses-paid conference in Tahoe."

"I haven't heard about any conferences in Tahoe."

"This isn't a law conference. It's well, a rites of passage conference for women turning fifty this year."

Bob was surprised. "You'll be fifty this year? I didn't realize. What's a rite of passage? Does it have something to do with midlife crisis?"

Kate grimaced. "It's called menopause, not a mid-life crisis. I don't know too much about it, but it sounded too interesting to pass up. Besides, it will do me good to be away for a few days."

Kate's lawsuit progressed steadily. She was pleased. Her only encounters with Ronald were legal ones, and there were always other people involved. She missed him at times, but she also felt he betrayed her.

One Saturday, Kate held a team meeting at her house to finalize the case.

"Plan to spend most of the day," she told her secretary, investigator, and two co-counsels. "We have a lot to do before we go to court next week."

While the team was outlining and planning strategy, the doorbell rang. Kate looked at everyone to see if anyone was expecting company, but they all shrugged.

She went to the door and opened it.

"Kathryn Chandler?" It was a short, bespectacled older gentleman.

"Yes. Who are you?"

"My name is Thomas Downing. Until today, I was head of research and development for P&G. After I finish talking with you, I'll be unemployed."

Kate was openly skeptical. "You're with P&G?"

"May I come in?"

"I...I guess so. We're having a rather important meeting."

"I'm sorry. I didn't know." He looked at the people sitting around the table. "Does this happen to be about the lawsuit?"

"Yes."

"Then this is the perfect time to tell you what I have."

Kate offered him a chair. "Just what is it?"

He hesitated and glanced at them. "I have documentation that P&G not only knew they were exposing some of their employees to toxic chemicals, but we carefully monitored the effects on our people for decades."

No one spoke. They were too stunned to reply.

Finally, Kate stood. "You're aware of what you're saying and that what you're doing could have serious ramifications for your company?"

"I'm aware of that," he nodded. "It's that I feel guilty about my part in it. I no longer feel what we did was right. I want to be able to live with myself. In the beginning, we thought we were helping people. Maybe we were. Somehow, we lost sight of our intentions."

He took several file folders from his briefcase and handed them to Kate. She flipped through them quickly.

"What is it?" her secretary asked.

Kate smiled. "Everything. He's got all the proof we need that the company experimented on some of its employees with everything from DDT to radiation."

James, one of the attorneys, stood. "Are you kidding? You mean all the things the workers said were true?"

"You didn't believe them?" Kate demanded.

"I wanted to, but I found it hard to accept that a company would intentionally do that to anybody."

Downing cut in, "There's also a file of people who died while working for P&G. Some of them may've died as a direct result of their exposure to various toxins."

"Can we have these documents? Will you testify for us?" Kate asked.

"Yes, if you subpoena me and the documents. They belong to P&G."

"Okay. Hold on. I'm going to call Bob and tell him about this. I'm sure we can get a subpoena today. I don't want to risk losing them. Everyone wait right here."

Kate went to the other room to call while her coworkers went through the files and discussed them. Kate came back in a few minutes.

"Mr. Downing, we need you to take these and go to your office. We'll be there within an hour to serve our subpoenas."

Later that night, Bob took Kate and her team out to dinner to celebrate. She felt wonderful.

She raised her glass in a toast to everyone. "Tomorrow, I begin work on a new set of motions and demands. We need to meet with P&G as soon as possible."

Bob nodded. "File your papers first thing Monday morning. I'll contact P&G's counsel and see if we can meet them Monday afternoon. You realize this will ruin them?"

"They should've thought about that before they decided to play God and use people as guinea pigs."

On Sunday, Kate was working on her new motions when the doorbell rang. She tried to ignore the intrusion, but the bell kept ringing. To her surprise, she answered and saw Ronald standing on the step.

"May I come in?" he asked.

"This is a bad time, Ronald."

"Busy with the stuff Thomas Downing gave you?"

"You know about that?"

"Who do you think sent him to you?"

Kate backed from the door. "Oh? You're the reason he confessed?"

"Please, may I come in for just five minutes?"

"Okay, five minutes."

Ronald walked in and sat on the couch in the living room while Kate sat in an easy chair across from him, staring.

"Well?" she asked.

"I've withdrawn from the case. In my talks with the P&G people, I discovered Downing. He told me about the documentation he had and how he felt guilty about it. I never saw any of it. I told him to do what his conscience directed. I also gave him your name and address and suggested he might want to talk with you."

Kate was stunned. "I'm supposed to believe that?"

"Why would I lie?"

"Because you discovered you have no defense in this case and you wanted to save your butt."

"My butt has been had," he sighed. "I made a mistake. I have already resigned. I'm sorry I ever got involved in this. Even more, I'm sorry I interfered with your case."

Kate stood and paced. "I'm glad you can admit your mistake. If you had something to do with Downing coming forward, I'm grateful. However, I'm still angry with you over the matter."

Ronald walked to her and held her hands. "I understand, and I don't blame you. I don't know if I can make it up to you, but I'd like to try. I love you very much."

She pulled free. "I don't know. I don't want to think about that right now. I need to devote all my energy to the case."

"I agree. I don't expect to hear from you until this is over, but I wanted to apologize and let you know how I feel. I don't want to give up on our relationship even though I made a huge mistake."

"Give me some time, Ronald. After this is settled, I'm taking a short vacation the first week in June at Lake Tahoe. We can talk when I return."

"Could I give you a ride or pick you up from the airport?"

"That would be fine," she smiled.

CHAPTER FIVE

The envelope read, *Denise Zaragoza, CPA, 94B San Antonio Way, Suite 203, Dallas, TX 75225.* The letters were gold-embossed, slightly raised, and beautifully scripted.

Denise's secretary looked briefly at the envelope, then she placed it on top of a small stack of mail and pressed the intercom button.

"Yes?" Denise asked.

"Mr. Atchison is here for his appointment, Miss Zaragoza."

"Thank you. Send him in."

Gene Atchison was a tall, slender man with gray hair. Denise had known him for years. She started doing his income tax returns the same year he opened his now-successful restaurant called Eugene's.

He flashed a wide grin as he sauntered through the door. Denise could've recognized that Texas smile from across the street.

"Good afternoon, Miss Zaragoza. It's wonderful to see you again."

Denise walked around her desk and hugged him. "Gene, you're being silly. It's good to see you, too, although it hasn't been that long."

"Every day I don't see you seems like an eternity."

Denise was embarrassed and playfully swatted his shoulder. "What do you have there?"

"Oh," he extended his arm. "Maria asked me to bring your mail in to you. I would've thought that during tax season, you'd be inundated with mail."

Denise laughed, accepted the mail, and dumped it on her desk. She straightened her black, pleated skirt. "You're the only one who thinks it's tax season. No one else starts in February. The mail won't get heavy until after April fifteenth. Until then, the IRS doesn't know we exist."

"I forgot."

Denise pulled up an extra chair close to the desk and motioned Gene to it. She took the other chair and kicked off her shoes as soon as she sat. As she looked down, she noticed one of the buttons on her red and orange floral blouse was undone, and she quickly buttoned it.

"So," she said. "How are you?"

"Not too bad, except I haven't seen you in a week."

"Gene, I thought you were here for tax purposes."

"I am, but you can't blame me for trying to mix business with pleasure. Besides, you know how I feel about you. I enjoy your company and would love to spend more time with you."

Denise sighed. "I know, Gene. I like you, too. I don't want to lead you on. I'm not sure I'm ready for a relationship."

"What is it this time?"

"Excuse me?"

"Every time I try to get close to you, you've got a reason why you can't spend more time with me. First, it was your grandmother who was ill, then she died. Then you wanted to lose weight before you could see me. Then you had knee surgery. Haven't you run out of excuses yet? You look great. I like you just the way you are."

"Gene, I don't know. I feel self-conscious about my weight."

"That's no excuse not to see me."

"What do you mean?"

"A good excuse would be because you don't like me, or you knew I was married, or you were interested in someone else. I'd accept one of those reasons. I know you have to eat dinner tonight, so say you'll come with me even if all you want is a salad."

Denise laughed nervously. "All right, already. I'll have dinner with you."

"Great, I'll pick you up at eight."

"Could we make it seven? I like to eat early."

"Seven it is." Gene was elated and didn't care what time they met. "Now, help me with my taxes so I don't pay them too much."

Denise took his file from the drawer. "You make so much money on that restaurant, it's hard not to have to pay. You need some write-offs or shelters. We'll work on that this year. How does your restaurant do so well?"

He grinned, "We make good food that people love to eat, then we charge a fortune for it."

"At least you're honest."

"Actually, I've been thinking of opening another restaurant in Houston."

"Gene, that's great! Be sure and keep track of expenses, even your time and mileage to Houston. What will you call it?"

"Eugene's of course. I don't want to confuse myself with another name."

Denise began shuffling papers. "Let's take a look at your figures and see what we can do. We need to start now for next year's return, especially if you open another restaurant. We want to save you all the money we can."

"I was hoping you'd say that."

When they finished going over all his records, Denise said, "That about does it. I have everything I need. I'll get started to-morrow. You may not have to pay much this year."

"Good. That way, I'll have more money to take you to dinner."

"We could go Dutch."

"No. I have someplace special I want to take you. My treat."

"You mean we're not going to Eugene's?"

"Not tonight. It's impossible to get reservations, and it's too expensive. I know a small, quiet place with great food and atmosphere."

As he walked out, he waved, "See you at seven."

After he left, Denise slumped in her chair and rolled her brown eyes. She liked Gene, but he was lean and trim. What could he see in her, so fat and squatty? She meant to start a diet. Her New Year's resolution had been to lose seventy pounds. Maybe she'd start after tax season.

She stood, picked up her shoes, and walked to the window. It stopped raining, but it was still gray and overcast. Denise looked forward to spring, but she somehow always missed it because of tax returns. By the time things settled down, and she felt human again, Texas was deep into its hot, humid summer.

She thumbed through the mail, setting aside some envelopes. After determining there was nothing important in the mail, she opened the one with gold lettering, being careful not to break her brightly-painted nails.

"Looks like an invitation," she chuckled. "Maybe this is the IRS's idea of a joke, inviting me to an audit."

Her forehead wrinkled as she read about the Rites of Passage Conference for women turning fifty.

"Holy cow. What's this? No one knows I'll be fifty this year."

She turned the card over, but the back was blank. She reached for the envelope and read the return address, then she made certain it was addressed to her.

"What is this? I never heard of such a castle. It must be a joke, but who do I know who'd do something like this? Why would they bother?"

Denise left work a short time later and drove the short commute home. Her shoes flew across the living room before she even closed the front door. She went to the kitchen and opened the refrigerator. There was some Chardonnay left, so she poured a glass.

When she sat on the couch, her cat, Tornado, took a flying leap into her lap, nearly spilling the wine.

"Hi, Torry. Have a good day? Me, too. Well, sort of. Remember the man I told you about named Gene?"

The tiger-striped cat with the cinnamon nose looked at her, yawned, and curled in a ball as if he was ready to hear a long story.

"Of course you do. I brought you leftovers from his restaurant."

Torry, who looked like he had consumed too many leftovers, shifted positions and sat back down.

"Gene's the one whose wife died a few years ago. He's been interested in me for some time, but I kept hoping he'd find someone else. He asked me out again tonight, and I said yes. He's a sweet man. I don't know what he sees in me."

Denise knew Torry wasn't listening. Even if he was, he didn't care about her mixed feelings for Gene.

"He's a gentleman and fun to be with," she added.

When she finished her wine, she went into the kitchen, followed closely by Torry. She fed him and took a shower. When she came into the bedroom, Torry was on the bed grooming himself.

"Good. You're here. Did I tell you I got a funny invitation in the mail today? It's for a three-day, expense-paid trip to some castle at Lake Tahoe. They must be selling something. You never get something for nothing, and it didn't say anything about a presentation."

She looked at Torry, whose head was hidden as he curled into a ball. "You have to help me. What do you think I should do?"

Denise got out the invitation and studied it again. Torry wasn't interested.

"Oh, what the hell. It won't cost anything to call. If they're up to something, I can always say no."

She dialed. While the phone rang, she sat on the edge of the bed petting Torry.

"Rites of Passage Castle. How may I help you?"

"Hi. My name is Denise Zaragoza. I received an invitation in the mail, and I was wondering what it's all about."

"I'm glad you called, Denise. My name is Julia."

"I only called, because I want to know more about this. What are you selling?"

"Nothing."

"Do I know you?"

Julia laughed. "No."

"Then how do you know me?"

"It's a long story. Trust me. I do know you."

"What's the gimmick behind the conference?"

"There isn't any. It's something new we're trying; the first rites of passage conference of its kind. We hope you'll want to be part of it."

"What's a rite of passage?"

"It's what we hope to accomplish. You'll meet with other

women who are turning fifty this year, and, hopefully, you'll come up with a way to help women achieve the respect and recognition they deserve."

Denise was skeptical. "How'd you know I'd be fifty this year? No one knows that. I even have my mother convinced I won't be fifty."

"You'll be fifty. You were born in July, 1945."

"Okay, okay," Denise was irritated. "What do I do to attend this conference?"

"Just say you'll come," Julia was jubilant. "I promise you won't regret it. We'll take care of everything. You'll come home a new woman."

"Is this a fat farm or health spa?"

"No. I meant you'd be new emotionally for the rest of your life."

"In that case, I'll try it. Can I leave if I hate it?"

Julia chuckled, "Of course. We're certain you won't want to leave, however. I need to know your choice of accommodations. We have penthouse suites, motor homes, bungalow cabins, and tents for camping."

Denise thought for a moment. "I'll take a cabin. Will I be sharing it with someone?"

"No. You'll have it all to yourself. We'll send further information. Air travel arrangements will be made for you. We're thrilled you'll be joining us."

"I hope I'm thrilled, too."

CHAPTER SIX

The doorbell rang. Denise was ready, knowing Gene would be on time. She liked that about him. She could always count on him to be punctual. Her mother was like that. They were never late for church, dental appointments, or school.

Denise wore one of her favorite outfits. She wasn't sure why she liked it, but she felt good in her black skirt and pale-pink blouse with a gray-and-black pin-striped blazer.

She looked at her reflection in the mirror. Maybe she liked the outfit because it made her look slimmer.

She opened the door. "Hi, Gene."

"You look ready. You also look great."

Denise blushed. "Thanks. Let me grab my coat."

Gene took her to a small Italian restaurant called Mario's. It was only large enough for twelve tables. Posters and prints of Italy adorned the walls. Each table had a checkered tablecloth and an empty Chianti bottle serving as a candleholder.

"I like this place," Denise commented. "It's warm and cozy."

Gene helped Denise with her coat and handed it to the waiter. At the table, he graciously held her chair for her.

"Glad you like it," he said. "I'm fond of it, because it never gets too crowded in here. Besides, they make the best lasagna in the world."

"Ohhh," Denise moaned. "That's one of the things I absolutely, positively shouldn't eat, but I love it. I don't need a menu. I'll have lasagna."

He smiled and ordered for both of them. He included a garden salad with house dressing and a carafe of wine.

During dinner, she looked at him and asked, "May I ask you something?"

"Sure. Anything."

"Why'd you get into the restaurant business? I know your wife wanted to have the business, but how'd you get started?"

He laughed and set down his fork. "You don't think I look the type?"

"As a matter of fact, you don't strike me as a high-class restaurant type. You like small, out-of-the-way places with homey atmosphere."

"Actually, I'm not the restaurant type at all. I was a salesman in pharmaceuticals. I didn't think I was too good at that, either."

She grinned. "I'll bet you were a tremendous salesman."

"Whatever. My wife didn't like all the traveling I did. She ate out often, because she didn't like cooking for one. What she liked most were cute little meat and potato places with exotic sauces and dressings. She knew she could cook as well as most of the places she frequented, so, one day, she found a place for sale and talked me into trying it with her."

"You've done very well."

"In the beginning, it was her doing. Her recipes and hard work got Eugene's off the ground. She even chose the name, saying it sounded like a great chef's place. I did the books, personnel, and ordered what she told me to get. She was the reason for its success."

"It's still working."

"After Gloria died, I considered getting out, but I didn't want to go back to sales work, and I knew she'd want me to keep the place. I hired some people to run the whole show. Now, I make so much money, I don't dare give it up. Maybe that's why I decided to open another one. Since I don't have much to do with the day-to-day operation, that'll give me something to do."

They ate in silence for a while. After Gene finished his dinner, he glanced at Denise. "May I ask you something?"

"Certainly."

"How come you never married?"

She gulped. She hadn't been expecting that. She couldn't decide if she was having a hot flash or just felt embarrassed. It was probably a hot flash.

"Well, it's...it's a long story."

"I have lots of time, and we'll order another cup of coffee. Besides, I want to know more about you. You seem sensitive and compassionate. You'd make someone a wonderful wife."

Now she was embarrassed. "Thank you. To be honest, I never married because I don't think I'm a very good judge of character in men."

"Are you kidding?"

"No. I made a big mistake once, and it almost cost me my life."

"I didn't know. I don't mean to pry, but I'm honestly curious."

Denise stared at him. She hadn't mentioned Derrick for twenty-five years. She hoped she never would have to. Still, there was something about Gene that made her feel it was all right to tell him.

"You really want to know?"

"Yes, I do."

"Well, after I graduated from high school, I went to college. I was good in math and wanted to be a CPA. There weren't many women in the program, so I thought it would also be a good place to find a man."

Gene chuckled, "Makes perfect sense to me."

"In my senior year, I met a man two years younger. I fell head over heels in love with him. He was gorgeous, bright, witty, charming, and, I thought, a perfect gentleman."

"He wasn't?"

"Not exactly. I wanted to be sure about him, so we dated for two years even after I graduated. I wanted to know him inside and out and make sure we were right for each other. He put up with all my doubts and concerns. He was patient and never pushed. Finally, when I was sure, I accepted his proposal and told my parents."

"You parents didn't like him, right?"

"Mom thought he was terrific. He had a good job, a promising career, and said all the right things. He came from a big family and told Mom we'd give her all the grandchildren she could want."

"And your father?"

"He was skeptical. All he would say was there was something about Derrick that didn't ring true, but he couldn't put his finger on it. Dad said he didn't want me to get hurt. Mom said he was upset, because he was losing his little girl. Dad gave his blessing, but he felt nervous about the marriage. He said if I ever needed anything, to call him."

"You never married Derrick?"

"No. It never got that far. The night before the wedding, his parents threw a huge rehearsal dinner at the restaurant they owned. There were lots of people there. We had most of the place to ourselves, because almost everyone was Derrick's relative. In the middle of dinner, three men stormed in and started shooting at the guests."

Gene was stunned. "My God! Why?"

"It turned out that all those people were part of an underworld family involved with drugs and other illegal activities. It all came out in the papers after the shooting."

"Were you hurt?"

"In more ways than one. I was shot in the right shoulder. It happened so fast, I don't remember much about it. Derrick grabbed me to protect me, then he was shot and died in my arms. Several other people were killed, too. My father was wounded, but he survived. He threw himself on Mom, who wasn't hurt."

"What a nightmare. So Derrick was.... How involved was he in the illegal stuff?"

"I never knew. He told me he was the bookkeeper for the family's various business interests, so he must have known. I had no idea what was going on, and I certainly didn't see any of his family after that."

"I don't blame you. It must've been terrible for you."

"It was. As soon as I was well, I left Chicago and moved to Texas."

"And your family?"

"They're still in Chicago. I don't see them too much, because I won't go back there. They come here occasionally to visit. I've been trying to get them to move. Since then, I've distanced myself from most everyone. It's easier than getting involved again."

"You've never been involved with anyone since?"

She smiled sheepishly. "Like I said, I don't trust my judgment in men. The only real relationship I've had in the past twenty-five years has been with food."

Gene was silent for a moment. "I didn't know. I hope I haven't been...."

She reached for his hand and held it. "Please, Gene. You've been sweet to me. You're the first man I've trusted in years. You didn't force me to tell you. I feel comfortable enough to confide in you. While you may have been persistent, you certainly haven't been pushy."

"God, I hope not. I'm not like the others."

"I know."

"So, do you have any interest in me?"

"I'm not sure," Denise replied. "There is something special about the way I feel toward you that I haven't felt for any other man, but I don't know how deep those feelings are. In some ways, you remind me of Dad. I even thought that when Gloria was alive. I loved how you were with her. It was always how I dreamed marriage would be."

They sat quietly for a while.

"Denise, this probably isn't the time to tell you this, but I planned to put my feelings on the table tonight," Gene said finally. "I had a hard time when Gloria died, and I always assumed I wouldn't find another woman I wanted to be with. In the past year, I found myself being drawn more and more to you. I might be in love with you."

"Oh, Gene, don't say that."

"I'm sorry, but that's how I feel. You're wonderful and special. I want to get closer. We have a lot to offer each other."

Denise tried to interrupt, but Gene raised his hand.

"No, let me finish. I won't push myself on you or even hint at a possible marriage, but I'd like to date you exclusively and see where it goes."

"I don't know, Gene."

"Why not? What have you got to lose? It's time to let go of the past."

"Well, I...."

"You know a lot about me having known me for ten years. You know I mean what I say. Are you interested in someone else?"

"That's not it. I'm frightened about letting myself care again."

He squeezed her hand. "Maybe it's time you did. Let someone care for you. You've punished yourself long enough."

Denise laughed as tears fell from her eyes. "Perhaps so. Okay, I'll date you, but I'm not ready for a commitment."

"Fair enough. All I want is a chance."

They finished their coffee. Gene paid the bill and they drove home. On the way, Denise told him about the invitation to the Rites of Passage Conference.

"Sounds like the chance of a lifetime. You're going, aren't you?"

"Of course."

CHAPTER SEVEN

The envelope read, *Kimberly Yamakara, Noe Middle School, 2906 Noe St., San Francisco, CA 94134*. The letters were gold-embossed, slightly raised, and beautifully scripted.

Kim pulled the envelope from her mailbox in the teacher's lounge.

"Must be some kind of school function," she thought. She glanced at the other mailboxes to see if the others had an invitation.

"They must've picked up theirs already," she reasoned when she saw hers was the only one. She lifted her backpack off her shoulders and stuffed the envelope inside.

"I can wait to see what it's about. School functions are boring," she yawned.

Kim grabbed her teal and periwinkle Eddie Bauer parka from the cubby at the end of the room and slowly slipped it over her light-blue sweater. She wrapped a brown scarf around her neck to protect it from the chilly air, and donned a matching stocking cap over her full head of black hair.

She looked out the window. It was still foggy and drizzly, but that was normal for the time of year. San Francisco could go the entire month of February without seeing the sun.

As she unlocked the door to her Explorer, a student ran into the parking lot.

"Miss Yamakara!"

"What is it, Stephanie?"

"You know that study on earthquakes they're doing in Parkfield?"

"Yes, what about it?"

"My dad said they're shutting it down."

"That's what I heard, too."

"But, you said we were going to take a field trip there to see how they predict earthquakes. How can we go if it closes?"

"Don't worry. It'll take six months before the project closes. I've been in touch with them, and they promised to get us in before they terminate the project."

"Oh. I didn't want to miss it. I'd love to learn how they predict earthquakes."

"You and several million other people. As soon as we have the details worked out, we'll be going. I'll let everyone know. I'm glad you're keeping up on things."

"Okay. Thanks, Miss Yamakara. Have a good evening."

"You too, Stephanie."

Kim climbed into her car and drove toward home. She enjoyed teaching seventh-grade science. The students were still eager to learn at that age, yet they were advanced enough that she didn't have to treat them like children. Her honors program in science finally caught on, and that year's class was one of the brightest she ever had. She loved the challenge.

The drive home wasn't long, but finding a place to park on her street always took more time. She and Linda cleaned out the small garage that was part of the first floor of their two-story home in the avenues, but it could only hold one small car. Since Linda's was smaller, she used the garage.

Kim circled several blocks and was ready to give up and double-park when she saw a car pull out near her house. She parked, stashed her backpack under her arm, and bounded up the stairs.

She threw open the front door and shouted, "Hi, Honey! I'm home!"

"For crying out loud," Linda complained. "I hate that expression. It sounds so...so Disney." She sat at the dining room table drinking a glass of orange juice.

"Well, excuse me." Kim dropped her backpack on the hall table. "Are we a little menopausal today?"

Linda stood and flailed her arms. "Oh, shit. I hate it. I'm fed up with hot flashes and mood changes. I hate the body changes, too, and I'm pissed at getting older. I'm tired of this crap. I'm going back to the doctor and tell her I want those drugs right now."

Kim walked over and kissed Linda's cheek. "It's a bitch, Honey. So when's your next appointment?"

"Not until next month." Linda sat down again. "If that teeny-bopper gynecologist doesn't give me the drugs then, I'll wring her neck."

"She's not a teenybopper." Kim got a bottle of mineral water from the refrigerator and carried it to the table.

"She's awfully young. She couldn't have started her own periods that long ago. Maybe if I threaten her, she'll give me something."

"That should do it."

"Sure, make fun of me. I'm serious. I want hormone therapy. I don't give a damn what my estrogen level is, I need it. I'm not myself. Everyone I've talked to says it helped."

Kim put her arms around her partner's neck. "I'm sorry. Tell her how you feel. You've been having a rough time."

"So when are you going to start being miserable, too? You're old enough. It's not fair I'm the only one suffering. You should suffer with me, then you'd understand."

Kim laughed. "Listen to you. How should I know when it'll happen to me? I'm only fifty this year. You're two years ahead of me. Every woman is different."

"Yeah, but I've been a bitch for two years already." She stood with her hands on her hips. "They say one of the best guides for when you're going to hit menopause is when your mother went through it. Do you know how old she was when it happened?"

"Who's they? I have no idea when or if Mom went through menopause. You know my family. They don't talk about things like that."

"Hell, your family doesn't talk to you at all. Maybe it's different for Japanese women. Maybe they aren't cranky. Maybe they don't get menopause. You should find out."

Kim grinned. "Don't be silly. All women go through it. It's just harder for some. That's what Gail says."

"Gail?"

"Gail Sheehy. Haven't you read that book yet?"

Linda hesitated, "Oh, yeah. *The Silent Passage.* I haven't had time."

"Great. I gave you that book more than a year ago. I'm not even into menopause, and I read it along with Germaine's book, the 250-most-asked questions book, and...."

Linda walked away. "I don't think reading about menopause will help me much. Do you think reading about a hot flash will make me toss and turn less at night when it hits? Will reading about it make you less grumpy when I kick off the covers, because I'm sweating like a pig? I doubt it."

"Okay. Let's talk about something else."

"You should call your mother and ask her when she went through menopause and if she was a bitch about it."

They laughed and walked into the kitchen, arm-in-arm, to fix dinner.

"By the way, where's Bailey?" Kim asked.

Linda snorted. "Bailey's tired."

"Tired?"

"I came home early, so I took him to the park for a run."

"You mean Golden Gate Park?"

"That's the one. He went bonkers and ran so much I almost had to carry him home. You should've seen him crawling up the stairs."

Kim went into the bedroom. Bailey wasn't on his bed. Then she saw the lump in the middle of her bed—under the covers.

"Bailey!"

The lump moved, then moaned.

"You aren't supposed to be under the covers."

In slow motion, Bailey slid his black head with its bloodshot eyes out from the top covers. Very deliberately, a small Labrador body inched out, barely disturbing the covers.

Once on the floor, the dog yawned, stretched, and slunk to his own bed a few feet away. He collapsed into it as if he just finished the Iditarod.

Kim smiled and walked back into the kitchen. "You'd have thought he ran all the way to the North Pole and back."

"Under the covers?"

Kim nodded.

During dinner, Kim asked, "How was your day?"

"Not too bad, although I get tired of firing people Mr. Hunter wants to get rid of."

"That's why they pay you the big bucks."

"I'd rather hire people and conduct seminars and training programs. That's supposed to be part of my job, too. Personnel directors aren't just for firing people."

"I'll bet you're good at it," Kim snickered.

"At what?"

"Seminars and training programs."

"Right. Anything exciting happen in your junior-science day?"

"Not much. Same old stuff, except I'm not giving any of my classes homework this weekend, because...."

"Don't tell me you finally got tired of grading papers?"

"No. Because everyone is studying for the big test next week."

"Good. Maybe you won't be spending the entire weekend on schoolwork."

Kim smiled. "Nope. I'm going to take most of it off. Of course, I have to spend some time writing the test, but I'm already started on that. I don't want to miss the party we're invited to." She paused, "That reminds me. I got some kind of invitation today, too."

"To what?"

"I don't know. I didn't open it. It's probably one of those dumb school things, although I haven't heard of anything coming up."

Linda grimaced, "I won't go with you no matter what it is. The last one was too much. Why don't you open it?"

Kim retrieved the envelope from her backpack and noted the return address was Lake Tahoe. As she walked back into the kitchen, she said, "I didn't notice until now that this is from Lake Tahoe."

Linda looked up. "Tahoe? Open it."

Kim opened the envelope and removed the invitation. Linda inspected the envelope.

"Read it out loud," she instructed.

"You are cordially invited to attend the first Rites of Passage Conference for women turning fifty. Three days and two nights, all expenses paid, at the beautiful Rites of Passage Castle on Lake

Tahoe. The goal of the conference is to establish a rite of passage for all future women turning fifty. Conference dates are June second through fourth. RSVP by April first for accommodation selection. Then there's an 800 number to call."

Kim looked at the back side of the card and found nothing. She glanced at Linda.

"That's it?" Linda asked.

"That's it. What is this?"

"It has to be a practical joke. Someone's planning something for your birthday."

"My birthday isn't until July."

"Well, it has an 800 number. Call it. Sounds intriguing. Do you think they're talking about that castle on the north side of the lake?"

"It's not a castle," Kim responded.

"Make sure you can take someone," Linda added.

"What do you know about this?" Kim asked suspiciously.

"Nothing, I swear. I'm as confused as you are. Call."

Kim hesitated, "I don't know, it sounds fishy."

"Go on. Where's your sense of adventure? What can it hurt to call? Come on. My curiosity is running wild."

Kim reached for the phone and dialed.

"Rites of Passage Castle. How may I help you?"

"I...I received an invitation today and...."

"Ah, Kimberly. I'm so glad you called."

"Who are you? How'd you know it was me?"

"I'm sorry. I didn't mean to be rude. I was just so happy you called. I'm Julia. I'm the one sponsoring the conference. I knew it was you, because all the other guests have called."

Kim didn't know what to say and finally uttered, "Oh."

"You'll come, won't you?"

"I don't know. What's this all about?"

"We're trying to establish a rite of passage for women turning fifty to help them achieve the recognition and respect they deserve."

"Sounds interesting," Kim said uncertainly. "Who's invited?"

"Women from all across the country."

"Why me?"

"We conducted an extensive search to find women from various ethnic, political, and professional backgrounds. Your name was selected."

"I suppose I should be flattered."

"We hope you'll join us. You won't regret it."

"Well, okay, I guess. What do I do?"

"Choose your accommodations. We have penthouses, bungalows, motor homes, and tents."

"I love to camp, I'll take a tent. Can I bring my partner and my dog?"

Julia hesitated. "This is just for you. We're flying everyone in."

"I'm not much of a flyer," Kim explained. "I'd rather drive. I'm just a few hours away."

"In that case, we'll send you a map showing where and when to meet us. You may bring Bailey. We'll see that he's comfortable."

"And my partner?"

"Not this time. This is something special for you."

"Okay, I'll wait to hear more."

"You'll be hearing from us."

Kim hung up and stared at Linda. "There's something funny going on here."

"Why do you say that?"

"She knew it was me when I called, and I only said I had a dog, but she knew Bailey's name."

CHAPTER EIGHT

The remainder of the school year passed quickly for Kim. Linda, her partner of fifteen years, finally received hormone therapy, and much of the turmoil at home settled down, but nothing helped the turmoil within Kim's family.

One day, Linda answered the phone. "Kim, it's your sister."

"Anna?"

"I didn't ask, but since you've only got one sister, I assume it's Anna."

Kim made a face and took the receiver. "Hello?"

"Hi, Kim. It's Anna."

"How are you?"

"I'm doing well, thanks. How about you?"

Kim's voice grew cold. "I'm fine, thank you. Why are you calling?"

"For goodness sake, Kim, don't be so skeptical. Do I need a reason to call?"

"You never call unless you want something."

"Okay, so I'm still upset about the trouble between you and Mom."

"Still? After all these years?"

"She isn't well, you know."

"Whoa, Anna. Don't try that on me. Whenever something isn't right with Mom, she develops mysterious medical problems, and everyone blames me. Is she sick and dying or not?"

"We're worried about her heart. She's not getting any younger, and you aren't helping."

Kim was irritated when she spoke, "No one in the family talks to me, but you all blame me for something that might be wrong with Mom? I don't need you to call and try that on me."

"I didn't call to blame you, Kim. I called to see if there was anything we could do to patch things."

"That's a commendable suggestion. Did you have anything specific in mind?"

"Well, Mom's birthday is coming up. We were thinking of throwing a party for her. Will you come?"

"Can I bring Linda?"

"Come on, Kim. You know that's what's upsetting Mother. She can't handle the fact that you're gay, and she certainly can't handle seeing you with Linda."

"I get it," Kim shouted. "You want me to come alone, never mention Linda, and pretend I'm not a lesbian."

"Would it hurt to just once do something for Mom's sake?"

"How will my pretending to be something I'm not help Mom?"

"Maybe if she thought you were straight, she'd take better care of herself instead of not caring if she lives or dies."

Kim was furious. "Anna, that's bullshit! If she doesn't want to live, then she doesn't want to. It's not my fault, and I can't change what she wants. But, I am who I am. Why don't you ask me to come and pretend I'm black, not Japanese? That would be easier. There's nothing wrong with me, and I won't change even for one day."

She took a deep breath and continued, "Linda and I have been together for fifteen years. It's about time someone in the family realized our relationship is solid. It is going to last. Mom actually liked Linda when they first met, then Mom found out we were a couple and started hating her. Mom hasn't spoken directly to me in eight years, and that hurts, Anna. I don't expect her to understand, but I expect her love and acceptance."

"She's worried about what people will think, about the disgrace this brings to the family. You know she disowned you and cut you out of her will, don't you?"

Kim swallowed, "No, I didn't know. I'm not surprised. As for the will, I don't give a damn about that."

"I think she's ready to mend some bridges, but she doesn't know how."

"It's easy to mend this bridge. All she has to do is pick up the phone and dial my number."

"Can't you call her?"

"I've tried calling her on her birthday for years. She hung up every time. She has returned all my letters, cards, and presents unopened. She even returned a letter to me from someone else. It came from San Francisco without a return address, so she thought it was from me. I'm sorry, Anna, but I gave up being rejected two years ago. I won't set myself up for that again. This time, she makes the first move."

"I know how you feel, Kim, but couldn't you try one more time?"

"All right. I'll send her a birthday card. If it comes back, I don't ever want to hear about this again. By the way, how's Dad?"

"He asks if I ever hear from you, but he makes sure Mom doesn't hear him ask. He misses you. His back injury has been bothering him, and he's been fighting with the Veteran's Administration over it."

"Why?"

"They say they can't verify it was a war injury. We think it's racial. They don't want to admit any Japanese men served in the Navy during World War Two."

"That's stupid."

"I know. There weren't many Japanese in the service, and the government doesn't want anyone to know about what they did. He suffers silently most of the time. He'd love to see you and Mom work things out."

"Have him work on Mom."

"You know Dad. Mom never gives him a chance to express his opinions."

"Then it's time he stood up to her. How's John?"

Anna sighed, "Now there's a work of art. He's still a butt head. He tells Mom he has only one sister. He says he won't lose his inheritance for a lesbian."

"Great family. I'm surprised he can even pronounce the word. So, why do you keep in touch?"

"You're my sister and I love you."

"Then why don't you try to help Mom mend her bridges?"

"Are you crazy?"

"No. If you love us both, why not work on her instead of me?"

"Mom still pays for my kid's dentist bills and some other things. I can't afford to alienate her and have her disown me, too."

"Thanks a lot, Anna. Did it ever occur to you that if all of us stood together, she might come around? Couldn't disown the whole family." She slammed down the receiver and stomped into the living room to slide into the recliner beside Linda.

"More family stuff?" Linda asked.

"Yeah, but I don't know what to do about it. I won't humor Mom by pretending to be something I'm not, and I won't go to a family gathering unless I can bring my family, too. Anna says it'll make Mom feel better. That's not my job."

Linda thought about that. "I'm not so sure. Would it hurt to let her think what she wanted? You don't have to lie and say you're straight."

"Don't you start. I'll be damned if she'll control my life like that. There's nothing wrong with being gay. I don't rub it in. It's her problem, not mine. She has to learn how to deal with it."

Linda laughed nervously, "Hey, I'm on your side. I just wanted to know where you stood. What are you going to do?"

Kim thought for a moment. "I told Anna I'd send Mom a birthday card, so I will. Maybe I'll resend some of the books she sent back without reading."

"Good idea. Maybe she'll read them this time."

Kim shook her head. "I won't get my hopes up."

Kim sent the card and two books written by the parents of homosexual children. To her surprise, they weren't returned. Kim wondered if Mom was reading them, or if Dad somehow intercepted them. There was no acknowledgment they were received.

The school year ended, and Kim was getting ready to go to Lake Tahoe for the mysterious conference. She considered calling her mother when she returned.

CHAPTER NINE

School let out two days before Kim was to leave. She cleaned out her desk before Friday, leaving the rest for when she returned. She looked forward to the weekend, even though she was a bit apprehensive and wondered what to expect.

"Do you have everything you need?" Linda spoke from the bathroom. She was preparing for work and hadn't paid attention to what Kim packed.

"Yes, Mother," Kim replied. "I'll only be gone two days. I won't need much."

"Cute," Linda sniped as she walked into the kitchen. "I only asked because they didn't tell you what to bring."

"That feels strange. I'm going camping while I'm there, yet I'm not taking a tent, sleeping bag, or anything. I can't believe they'll provide me with everything I need. Oh, well, it's only a couple of days. If I don't like it, I can always move into the penthouse."

"You have Bailey's things, including his smoking jacket for the penthouse?"

"Yes, Linda. We have everything. He's taking food, water, leash, cow hooves, and toys. Actually, he's taking more than I am."

"When are you leaving?"

"Around nine. We'll miss the traffic and still get there early enough for Bailey and me to take a hike before meeting the others."

"Where are you meeting?"

"At the airport. The others are coming in on a private jet. You know, that airstrip just outside of town."

"Oh, yeah," Linda mumbled, giving Kim a hug. "How many will be there?"

"They never said."

"Please be careful and drive safely. If you need anything, call. I have an address and phone number where you'll be, don't I?"

Kim shrugged, "I left the 800 number by the phone, but the only address I have is the post office box."

"I'm sure you'll have a great time. You need the break. I can't wait to find out what this is all about."

"Me too." Kim kissed Linda and waved as her partner left for work.

The drive to Lake Tahoe was perfect. The weather was warm, without being too hot. Even the Sacramento Valley was tolerable. Traffic was light. Kim loved watching the rushing creeks and rivers gush past, bulging with spring melt from the winter snows.

She turned off near Echo Summit and drove several miles into the woods. She and Bailey hiked on one of their favorite trails, stopping near a small lake for lunch. It was Kim's first trip to the Sierras since fall, and she wondered what kept her away so long. Reluctantly, they hiked back to the car and began the short drive to the airport.

Kim arrived fifteen minutes ahead of schedule. She could see the airport from Highway 50, but she had never been there.

"Well, Bailey," she told the dog sleeping in the back seat, "we're early. Let's stretch our legs."

She climbed out of the car, and Bailey sat up. A slight breeze blew, and the air seemed cool, so she slipped on a long-sleeved sweater. She was glad she wore Levi's, not shorts.

Kim and Bailey walked toward one end of the runway. It was a small airport. Large planes could never land there.

As they walked, she spoke to Bailey. "I'm not sure why I'm here. This whole thing seems strange, and I've had an eerie feeling all day. It's almost as if we aren't really here. I'm glad you're with me. It makes me feel safer."

Bailey wasn't listening. He was busy chasing lizards and chipmunks. Kim looked back at the airstrip. It was deserted. As she started walking toward the mass of concrete, a long, silver limousine pulled in and parked near her Explorer. The driver got out, checked Kim's license plate, and returned to the limousine.

Kim walked faster. When she heard a plane coming in, she looked up and saw one approaching the runway.

"Come on, Bailey, step on it. Looks like the show's about to begin."

By the time they reached the car, the plane was rolling down the runway. It looked like a Lear jet.

"Excuse me," a voice said, "but are you Kim Yamakara?"

She spun and found herself face-to-face with a female driver. "Yes, I am."

"I'm happy to meet you. I'm Hildy. This must be Bailey." She stooped to pet him. He sniffed her, then licked her hand. Hildy took a dog treat from her pocket and gave it to him.

Kim decided Hildy was okay. Otherwise, Bailey would've barked at her. She had long since learned to trust his instincts with people. When he barked, Kim stayed away from that person.

"I'm here to meet everyone and escort you to the castle," Hildy said. "The others are on the plane."

They watched the plane taxi closer and stop. The door opened, and a woman pilot lowered the stairs.

"Hi, Jan," Hildy said. "Have a good flight?"

"Couldn't have been better. The weather was perfect, and we made record time. Why don't you help these women with their things? Someone must've told them they were staying three months, not three days."

An African-American woman emerged from the plane. "Most of the bags belong to Marge," she motioned.

Another woman stuck her head out and added, "We think she brought her saddle and horse, too."

Marge finally stepped down and said, "I needed an extra bag for my cosmetics."

Hildy turned to Kim and laughed. "As soon as we get them unloaded, we'll do the introductions and head for the castle."

Kim nodded and watched the two women disappear into the plane. It was a good touch to have a woman chauffeur and pilot. Kim began to wonder if she'd see any men at all during the conference. She watched patiently as three women, followed by what seemed to be hundreds of suitcases, come out. Then came Hildy and Jan.

"I might as well make the introductions," Hildy said. "You know Jan, your pilot. I'm Hildy, your chauffeur. This is Kim Yamakara—I hope I pronounced your name correctly. The others are Marge Sinclair, Denise Zaragoza, and Kate Chandler."

"That's it?" Marge asked. "Only four of us for this conference? I knew there was something fishy about this."

"How many were you expecting," Hildy asked.

"I don't know, but I certainly thought there would be more than four."

Jan laughed. "As long as they have the best four, they don't need anymore."

"Where are you from?" Kate asked Kim.

"San Francisco. I drove up, but it's pretty close, and I hate to fly. This is my dog, Bailey."

"You brought your dog?" Marge questioned.

"What's the matter, Marge?" Denise teased. "Didn't you ask if you could bring a dog, too?"

"I never thought about it," Marge admitted. "I'm from North Dakota. Denise is from Texas and Kate's from New York. Looks like this Julia character really spread us out."

They shook hands and exchanged greetings, eyeing each other inquisitively. Marge complained about the long flight, her boots being too tight, and wearing good clothes. Kate tried to figure out what time it was in Lake Tahoe and New York. Denise was busy trying to remember what she forgot.

Hildy smiled. "Don't worry about forgetting anything. Julia will take care of everything you need. She's your hostess for the weekend. I'm sure you're anxious to meet her."

"I'm anxious to see this castle," Marge put in.

A Jeep drove up. A young man got out, ran to Jan, and hugged her off her feet.

She smiled and looked at the group. "You won't be needing me anymore, so I'll be going. I have plans for the weekend. See you on Sunday."

Jan waved, then she and the young man climbed into the Jeep and drove away.

Once all the luggage was loaded into the limousine, Marge, Denise, and Kate took seats.

Hildy turned to Kim. "Follow us. The castle isn't far."

They left the airport, drove a short distance on a paved road, and then turned left onto a narrow dirt road that wound through the forest as if looking for a place to go.

"You know, Bailey," Kim said, "there's something strange going on here. I can't put my finger on it, but whoever heard of a conference with only four women, and such women! Christ, they couldn't have found four more different women if they tried."

Kim looked in the rearview mirror. Bailey sat up with his head sticking out the open window.

"I know you're listening," Kim said. "You may not understand what's going on, but I'm not sure I do either. Look at us—a tall, blonde contractor from North Dakota, a gorgeous fashion-model attorney from New York, an overweight Hispanic accountant from Texas, and a Japanese lesbian schoolteacher. Weird."

Then it hit her. "Bailey, there's no dust. We're on a dirt road, following a limousine, and there's no dust in our faces! This is odd."

They traveled for fifteen minutes when the limousine turned around a large bend in the road, and a clearing appeared with a castle sitting in it.

"My God! Look at that, Bailey. I never knew there was such a thing like it at the Lake. I've never seen anything like it. It looks like something out of a Disney movie."

Kim sat in her car and stared at the magnificent building. There was no moat or towering turrets. It was made of huge stones of different colors—pink, beige, blue and lavender. There were two gigantic doors in front and bigger windows on either side of them. Kim couldn't see the sides or the back.

Finally, she climbed out of the car. The other women stood around the limousine, gaping.

"What the hell is that thing doing in the middle of a forest?" Marge asked.

"That's the Rites of Passage Castle, where you'll have your conference," Hildy noted. "Pretty impressive, eh?"

"I'll say," Kate replied. "I can honestly say I've never seen anything like it."

"You never will," Hildy added.

"How big is it?" Denise asked.

Hildy smiled. "No one knows for sure. It never seems to end."

Kim eyed Hildy skeptically. "What kind of comment is that? Someone built it. There must be a floor plan."

"It must be more than four thousand square feet," Marge suggested.

"It's a lot more than that," Hildy answered. "You're only seeing the front."

"Good guess, Contractor," Kate said, nudging Marge.

"Let's get our stuff and get on with this," Denise said.

"Leave everything in the limo for now. We'll see that it's taken to your rooms. You have business inside."

"Business?" Denise queried.

"Yes. Come in. Let me show you around and introduce you to your hostess."

They entered the lobby. It was colorfully decorated with large swooping drapes of blue and lavender, crystal chandeliers, marble floors, brass fixtures, and plants hanging everywhere.

"That's the main desk," Hildy pointed to an enormous mahogany desk taking up one side of the lobby. "If you need something, there'll always be someone there to help you."

"How come no one's there now?" Marge asked.

"Do you need anything?"

"No."

"When you do, someone will be there."

The women eyed each other.

"I need to show you a few things before you meet Julia," Hildy continued. "Over there is Room Five. Julia will explain its significance later. This way is a circular hall. As we walk around it, you'll notice five doors leading off it. Four will have your names on them."

Hildy led the way and opened the one with Kim's name on it. "They're identical, small, office-like rooms. You'll be using these when you do your assignments."

"The room's empty," Kim observed.

Hildy closed the door. "Don't worry. You'll have them filled soon enough."

"What's the fifth door for?" Marge asked.

"That leads to the main conference room where you're going right now to meet Julia. Each of your offices are on the outside of that room, and you can enter from either the conference room or the hall. Now, if you don't mind, I'll take you to the conference room."

She opened the remaining door, and the women walked in. The room was almost bare. There was a table and small podium at one end, but there were no windows, and the only doors leading out, went to their offices or the hall. Behind the podium were blue and white curtains covering the entire length of the room.

In the center of the room was a round table with four chairs. The women walked around aimlessly, not sure of what they got themselves into, but anxious to meet Julia.

"Please have a seat," Hildy directed. "Julia will be with you in a moment."

The women sat. Kim turned to ask Hildy a question, but she'd already left.

CHAPTER TEN

"Good afternoon, Ladies. My name is Julia Worthington. I'm your hostess for this conference, and I'm thrilled all of you could make it. While I'll be happy to entertain questions at the end of the session, I'd like you to pay special attention to what I have to say first."

An elderly woman moved slowly across the room toward the podium. She had a slight spring in her step which made the skirt of her floral-print dress sway. Soon, she stood in front of the podium and leaned her slim elbows on it.

"I hope you haven't become too comfortable in this room, because, while it looks like a typical conference room, I find it a bit stuffy." She brushed loose strands of white hair from her forehead.

She eyed the women sitting silently in their chairs and smiled. "I assure you, this will not be a typical conference. You'll probably never attend anything like it again in your life."

The women shifted uneasily in their seats, wondering what to expect from their hostess, who appeared to be at least thirty years older than they.

Everyone's eyes were on the petite woman. Her blue eyes danced with enthusiasm as she surveyed the group. Julia removed the podium from the table, walked over, and slid it through the curtain.

Then she spun on her toes, as if fearing she'd lose their attention. "We need a more pleasant environment in which to conduct our business. One of the nice things about this castle, as you'll soon discover, is that we can have anything we want, even in our conference room."

As she started opening the curtain, she said, "I like a conference room with a lovely garden setting—lush green grass, trees, shrubs of all kinds, and flowers of every color."

From behind the curtain emerged a beautiful tropical garden loaded with trees of all sizes, and a wide variety of flowers. The women were stunned.

"Where the hell did that come from?" Marge said, jumping to her feet.

"I thought we were in a building," Denise added.

Julia barely cracked a smile. "Pretty amazing, isn't it? Let your imaginations run wild. What would you like to see in our conference room?"

She motioned to them. The women stood and walked forward slowly, drawn toward the garden.

"Okay, I'll play," Kim shouted. "How about a waterfall?"

Kate laughed nervously. "Oh, my God, there it is! This is unbelievable. I think we should add a stream so the water from the falls has someplace to go."

Julia watched silently as the women wandered into the garden. A small stream gurgled along the side of the path. It led away from the waterfall and vanished in the distance.

Marge got down on her hands and knees. "This is real dirt, grass, and look! There are even tiny mushrooms growing over there. Who asked for those?"

Julia beckoned the women to follow her. As they did, Kim looked back and saw the room they just left had disappeared.

"Wait a minute," Kim said. "Where's the conference room?"

The others were equally astonished, but Julia didn't look back to explain. "It's still there, and you can bring it back any time you want. All you have to do is ask for it, and it'll be there. This, however, is my idea of a conference room."

She waved her arms and took a deep breath. "Clean fresh air and the freedom to commune with nature and be ourselves. That's a special feature of this castle. If you verbalize what you want, it's there—within reason, of course. We'll get to that later."

Julia arrived at a small clearing in the garden. "I'd like to see a lovely blue gazebo with a cute yellow and white table and chairs so we can continue our discussion."

The women eyed each other again as the gazebo came into view. Marge held back, not sure she wanted to be involved in something so strange.

Kate turned to her. "What's the matter, Marge? Frightened?"

"Hell, no." She thought about her answer and added, "Yes, a little. Don't tell me you aren't apprehensive about what's going on here. This isn't normal."

"Yeah," Denise said. "Hold on a minute, Julia. Don't you think you should give us some idea of what's going on?"

"That's just it," Julia replied. "Nothing's going on, except what's in your mind or imagination. Free yourselves from your old habits and ways of thinking. Live a little and have some fun with this. Be a child again. You'll never have another opportunity to be this free as long as you live."

Denise pulled out a chair and sat down. "Okay, Julia. We're here, and it's your meeting. Come on, Girls. Let's play a little. It could be fun, and it definitely will be interesting."

The others reluctantly came forward and sat at the table.

Kim looked around. "I don't hear any birds."

Immediately, a meadowlark landed on a branch near her and sang. The women jumped, then laughed.

"Now you're getting the idea," Julia grinned. "Would anyone care for something to drink?" She took a seat with her guests.

Marge raised her hand. "How about a beer? I'd love a cold

Michelob."

A young blonde woman in gray slacks, a long-sleeved flowered blouse, and cowboy boots walked up to the table and placed a bottle of Michelob in front of Marge.

"Would you care for a chilled glass?" she asked.

Marge's eyes widened. "No, thanks. I'll drink it from the bottle."

"As you wish." She left.

"Wait a minute!" Kate called. "How about me? I'd like a Chevas and water."

A tall, young, African-American woman, dressed the same as the first woman, but without the cowboy boots, strolled to the table and set a small bottle of scotch next to Kate. She smiled and placed a glass of ice and a carafe of water next to it. She left as quickly as she came.

"There's magic in this castle," Julia said, "and within each of you. You'll soon discover that each of you has a young woman at your disposal to serve your needs and be of assistance whenever you need it."

She turned to the other two women. "If you'd like to meet your personal guides and order something, please do so. Then, we'll continue with the indoctrination."

"I'd like orange juice," Denise said.

"I'll have mineral water," Kim added.

A young Japanese and young Hispanic woman joined the table to deliver the drinks.

"I can't believe this," Kim said. "It's almost as if they knew what we wanted before we did."

Julia stood. "Now that I have your attention, perhaps we can begin. The first thing I want to tell you is, I'll be one hundred years old this year, not fifty like the rest of you."

"Really?" Marge gasped. "I never would've guessed you were that old."

Julia smiled. "Thank you. I'm proud of my age and how I look and feel. I can honestly say it feels wonderful to be one hundred, of good health and sound mind, although I'm certain you're questioning that last part.

"When I turned fifty, the year you were born, I decided it was time to take care of myself if it wasn't too late. I spent a lot of time and energy preserving the things about myself that I could. You'd do well to follow suit."

The women were impressed as Julia walked and talked. The bounce in her step wasn't that of a woman her age, although none were certain just how a woman of one hundred should walk. She stood tall and didn't stoop at all.

"When I celebrated my fiftieth, I became extremely cold and bitter toward a world that treated me like a has-been. I was a nobody, an old hag who was at the end of her life. I didn't feel that way. I felt I was at the beginning of a new life, but I also felt empty because no one recognized what I had accomplished and that I still had so much more to offer.

"I was treated like something less than a woman, because menopause robbed me of my child-bearing years. Yet, without that worry on my mind, I had more time and energy to devote to other interests. Alas, society cast me aside, hoping I wouldn't be a burden in my advanced years."

She became more dramatic as she walked around the table, gesturing and making the women's heads turn to follow her movements.

"We celebrate many things in our lives—births, marriages, bar mitzvahs, graduations, promotions, and even deaths. There's nothing to celebrate when a woman goes through menopause. I don't think any of us threw a party when we started having our periods, yet, that's when society said we became women. I say, we truly become women when we stop having those blasted periods, so why not celebrate that?"

Everyone was silent. She stopped walking and leaned over the table. "Isn't fifty the perfect time to celebrate? We're free of the things that have been expected of us, and we're mature enough to know ourselves. It's the time for a rite of passage, for us to tell the world we have arrived, are to be reckoned with, and are heading toward the best we'll ever be."

"Is that where we come in?" Denise asked. "We're here to work on a rite of passage?"

Julia nodded. "Precisely. It has always been a fantasy of mine that there should be such a rite. Now it's time to develop one. You've been chosen to plan one that, hopefully, will live for generations, being passed down from mother to daughter, to become part of every woman's life when she turns fifty. This should be something a woman looks forward to."

"I'm a little confused," Kate admitted. "Are we really supposed to come up with something, or is this just fantasy?"

Julia laughed. "Good question. Everything you experience this weekend will be fantasy. Have a good time with it. The rite of passage you develop will be real."

The women were speechless, afraid to look at each other. Marge feared to finish her beer, because she felt certain it was spiked with something. Denise wondered if hot flashes brought on hallucinations. Kim was convinced she was in the middle of the best dream she ever had. Kate frantically ran through her list of friends to see if anyone was capable of such an elaborate joke.

Julia was undaunted. "You'll be given specific assignments while you're here, and you'll be expected to do certain things. You'll also have plenty of free time in which to do them and still have fun. You can think, explore, play, enjoy your vacation, and search your inner selves. No expense has been spared to insure your good time and well being."

No one knew what to say.

"No matter what you do or where you go for these three days, you'll never leave the grounds of this property. You'll always be safe. You have four young women always at your disposal. But, you will not be able to tell anyone in the next three days why you're here."

She sat and faced her audience. "Please, finish your refreshments and walk a bit to stretch. Then, I'll throw this open to questions. I'm sure you won't fully comprehend what's happening here until long after you've left. Don't be worried if you don't understand everything now."

CHAPTER ELEVEN

"Does anyone have a question?" Julia asked.

"Yeah," Marge answered. "Why us, and why only four?"

Julia nodded. "We were looking for women who were very diverse ethnically, geographically, socially, and so on. You have to admit, we did a good job in finding four completely different women."

"No kidding," Kate chuckled. "How'd you find us specifically?"

"Through a computer search. We fed it what we were looking for, then when we had a list of names, we made further refinements on the selection."

"Like what?" Kim asked.

Julia hesitated. "All right. I'll be honest about some of the criteria. You're all within five IQ points of each other. You're not considered geniuses, but you're bright. We thought having a common intelligence level would help you communicate and work well together despite your other differences."

"That's it?" Denise asked.

"We also looked for women who were going through difficult times in their lives."

"What do you mean?" she shot back.

"I don't need to explain each individual's particulars, but if you each take a good look at your personal, private, professional, and emotional life, you'll know what I mean. If you want to share those things with each other, that's up to you."

Kate was nervous. "You mean all that's in a computer somewhere?"

Marge was irritated. "Come on. How can you know if any of us have problems?"

"That's not important," Julia said.

"I think it is. Your computer can tell you I've been cheating on my husband? I don't believe it."

Julia looked into Marge's eyes. "I believe his name is Greg."

Marge was flabbergasted. "Jesus! What kind of hoodoo show is this? Not even my husband knows his name. Do you know everything about me?"

"The point is," Julia continued, "I'm not here to judge or condemn you. All I'm saying is that each of you is struggling with something major in her life right now. That was one of the things we were looking for."

"Why?" Kim asked.

"Because I believe that makes you more aware of what's going on in the world around you. It makes you more sensitive to your own and other women's struggles. If everything in your lives were fine, you probably wouldn't want to be here. Besides, I felt you could use a three-day vacation without a care in the world."

Kate smiled. "Okay, you've got a point, but do you really think that will help us develop a rite of passage? I'm not even sure what one is."

"That's why you're here and it's not imperative you know what a rite of passage is," Julia nodded. "I'm not certain anyone knows. It's all up to you."

"What if we don't come up with one?" Kate suggested.

"You will."

"Or what?" Marge challenged.

"Don't be hostile, Dear," Julia replied. "There's no or what with this. Trust me. I have faith in you that you'll find an answer."

"I'd like to know something." Denise raised her hand. When

we landed at the airport, I was certain my watch showed three o'clock. It still does. It hasn't moved. Did you have anything to do with that, or is my watch broken?"

The others looked at their watches. All had stopped at three o'clock.

"I confess we did have something to do with that," Julia admitted. "We thought if you didn't have to worry about time during your stay here, we could accomplish more. There will just always be enough time for you to do what you want. It will make it seem like more than three days."

"How'd you do it?" Denise asked.

Julia laughed, "Trade secret."

"I like knowing what time it is," Marge complained.

"Don't worry, Marge. You'll be happy later that you didn't know the time."

Denise raised her hand again. "Okay. Let's say we have three fun-filled fantasy days here, and we come up with a rite of passage. What happens when we leave? You said we wouldn't be able to tell anyone why we're here, so what happens to the rite of passage?"

"That's a good question," Julia responded. "If you recall, I said you wouldn't be able to tell anyone while you're here. Part of the development of a rite of passage has to be how to get the message to the rest of the world. I hope you'll do that."

Kate snickered, "We figured we'd leave that up to you and your computer. You found us, know all our secrets, and seem willing to grant all our wishes. You must have a better network than Santa Claus, or do you do that, too? You could spread the results of our findings all around the world."

"I think you've got it, Kate," Marge put in. "She is Santa Claus and can deliver the rite of passage to all women at Christmas."

Julia walked over to Kate and patted her on the back. "See? You're already starting to think about it. There are many resources available to you while you're here. Assume for now, there are no limits. Don't expect me to do it for you, or I would've already done so and saved the expense of bringing you here.

"This is for you and other women who'll be turning fifty. I've had my day. Feel free to call on me and my resources anytime. I can be found by calling out my name and coming to room five off the main lobby."

Julia continued walking while the women sat quietly. "Ladies, I'm sure you'll have more questions as we continue. Feel free to ask them anytime. Your personal guides will be able to answer many of your questions. They are here for your use. They'll show you to your quarters. Get to know them. They can be very helpful."

"Do they have names?" Kim asked.

Julia grinned. "Of course. They're your main link to everything that happens this weekend."

"Hildy showed us some offices in the hall with our names on the doors," Denise noted. "What are those for?"

"Oh, yes. I almost forgot. Those offices will be for your personal use as you begin working on the rite of passage."

"But they're empty," Kim added.

"When you retire to those rooms to work, you'll be allowed to decorate them in any way you please. Equip them with whatever you need and furnish them so that they become workrooms for your enjoyment and comfort. Your personal guides will assist you."

"What do you have planned for us this weekend?" Marge asked.

"In a few minutes, your guides will show you to your rooms. Dinner will be served in two hours in the main dining room, which is on the other side of the lobby."

"Since our watches don't work," Marge stated, "how'll we know when two hours have passed?"

"When you're hungry, it'll be time."

Denise nudged Kim. "The computer can even tell when we're hungry."

As the women stood, Julia turned. "Oops, I almost forgot. What do you want for dinner?"

"What's on the menu?" Denise asked.

"Whatever you want."

Marge waved. "This might not be so bad after all. I was afraid this would turn out to be one of the health resorts that serve tofu and salad. I want a T-bone steak, salad with thousand island dressing, and a baked potato with the works."

Kim grinned. "You're serious? We can have anything? I'll take lobster and a crab salad."

"I want a Michelob with my meal," Marge added.

Julia turned to Kate, who shrugged.

"I don't know. I guess I'll have pork tenderloin, a spinach salad and wild rice. This is fun."

Denise thought hard. "I almost don't know how to order without a menu."

"What do you like to eat?" Kim asked.

"I'd like a tossed green salad with blue cheese dressing, and a nice pasta with scallops or shrimp. Both, if I can have them."

Julia nodded.

"What kind of sauce on your pasta?" Kim teased.

"You know, a light sauce. Light on oil, heavy on garlic."

"It's a good thing you don't have a date tonight," Kate pointed out.

CHAPTER TWELVE

Marge reached down and grabbed her beer, draining the bottle. She looked at the others. "I'm ready. Where's that little maid who's supposed to take care of me?"

The tall blonde who had served her beer, tapped her on the shoulder. "Right behind you, Marge, and if you don't mind, I'm your guide, not your maid. If you're ready, I'll show you to your quarters."

"Excuse me. I wasn't sure what to call you. I believe I have the penthouse. This whole thing is a bit confusing. I don't know what to think."

"That's obvious," the guide muttered. "Come with me. Maybe I can shed some light on things."

Marge smiled. "Great. Do you have a name?"

"Call me Maddie." She led Marge out of the garden and into the castle.

"I need to get my stuff," Marge said.

"All your things are in your suite. I moved it for you. How long did you plan to stay?"

Marge laughed. "Maybe I overpacked a little. You said suite?"

"You requested the penthouse, didn't you? A penthouse is more than one room. With all the stuff you brought, that's a good thing."

Maddie went to the elevator in the lobby and pressed the up button.

Marge chuckled, "Now, here's where I get confused again.

You see, when we drove up, I could've sworn this building wasn't any more than three stories high. It's not the kind of building that needs an elevator. Plus, I'm a contractor. I build buildings. This one isn't tall enough to have a real penthouse."

The elevator door opened, and Maddie gently pushed Marge inside. "Let me explain something to you, Margie. You need to drop the attitude. You requested a penthouse; you'll have a penthouse. You can do almost anything you want this weekend, at no expense to you. A lot of time and energy went into making this conference a success. The sooner you just accept things and go along with the program, instead of questioning everything, the sooner you can enjoy yourself and figure things out."

"All right. You don't need to lecture me. Don't call me Margie."

The door closed.

"Push the button marked P," Maddie instructed. "It'll take you to the penthouse. When you come back down, L takes you back where you started. Got it?"

"What about the other buttons?" Marge touched P with authority.

"You can punch them until your brains fall out, but all you'll ever get in this elevator is the penthouse or the lobby. None of the other floors are available to you."

"Right." She looked around. "Like the elevator will know if it's me or you pushing the buttons?"

Maddie sighed, "You don't have the access code for the other floors."

"What's on them?"

"You don't need to know. Now stop giving me a hard time."

"Okay."

The elevator slowed and stopped. The door opened onto a

large entry hall with a gold and white carpet that glittered in the light of a large chandelier hanging overhead. The walls were papered with a white brocade pattern containing hints of blue and mauve.

"This is beautiful," Marge stated. "Is this where I'm staying?"

Maddie pointed. "Right over there through those double doors."

"The one's with the gold M's on them?"

Maddie nodded.

"Is that for my name?"

"Of course. It's a little touch to appeal to your ego."

Marge beamed. "I like that. You must've known I would. Does anyone else have a penthouse?"

"You're the only one."

They walked forward, and Maddie opened the double doors. Marge was stunned. She never stayed in a penthouse before, and she only imagined what it would be like. She never saw anything so huge and beautiful. Everything matched—carpet, drapes, wallpaper, and expensive furniture.

"There's no bed," Marge observed.

"This is the living room. Come on. I'll give you a tour. In addition to the living room," Maddie opened another door, "you have a private bath. Through that door is a pool and jacuzzi, plus a workout room. Off the middle of the living room is a fully stocked kitchen. You probably won't need it, but I'm sure it has gadgets you never heard of, all high-tech."

"Hell, I don't cook much." She looked into the kitchen and whistled.

"I don't either. That's one thing you can ask of me that you won't get."

Marge walked to the refrigerator and opened it. "Great! It's stocked with my kind of beer, and there are things for sandwiches and midnight snacks."

"I understand midnight snacks are a big item with you."

Marge glanced at her guide. "I was going to ask how you knew, but never mind. You seem to know a lot about each of us. For your information, I don't sleep well. I have a lot on my mind, and menopause keeps me awake. I usually get up and go to the kitchen table to think things out, and I snack. I do my best thinking then."

"Does it help?"

Marge laughed, "Not really, but it makes me feel as if I'm trying."

Maddie opened another door. "For the last part of your suite, behold the bedroom."

Marge's arms flew up. "My God! This is some bedroom. I love it. A circular bed. I always wanted to sleep on one."

She bounced on the bed. "Perfect mattress, too. Does it have one of those vibrating massagers built in?"

Maddie grimaced. "I doubt it, but, if you want one, ask for it."

"What are all those buttons for?" Marge looked at an array of knobs on a panel near the headboard.

"There's an explanation sheet beside the bed."

Marge squealed with delight and pushed various buttons, changing the ceiling from normal to an open-air view, to mirrors, then to a chandelier. Another button brought out a giant television screen. There was one for a wet bar, one for music, one for lights. She decided to try the other buttons later.

"I'll have fun with this," she giggled.

"No doubt," Maddie shrugged.

"Does a man come with the room?"

"You'll find everything you need or want."

They walked back to the living room.

"Unless you need something else, I'll leave now," Maddie said. "Have fun. Your things have been put away. Take time to freshen up. When you're ready, come down for dinner."

Marge looked at her watch. "How'll I know when it's time?"

Maddie smiled. "Don't worry. Whenever you're ready, come down. That's when it's dinnertime. If you need anything in the meantime, holler, but don't keep me jumping too much. Do a few things for yourself."

As the door closed, Marge stuck out her tongue. "Who does she think she is? I don't need a maid. I can take care of myself, even here. I sort of like her. She reminds me of myself when I was younger. Besides, she's the only one here I can talk to."

She turned on the CD player. It was loaded with some of her favorite country-western music. She opened the drapes and marveled at the view of the lake, but she was still puzzled.

"I must be at least fifteen stories up for a view like this. There's no way I could see this much of the lake from only three stories. I don't understand."

She moved to the wet bar, got a beer, and poured some into a chilled mug. She took her drink onto the balcony and sat in one of the comfortable lounge chairs. She surveyed the countryside, looking for landmarks, but nothing stood out except the lake.

She finally checked the closets and dressers and found her things neatly hung or carefully arranged in drawers.

As she headed for the bathroom to take a shower, she glanced at the entry doors. She didn't remember seeing any other doors in the hall, but she opened and looked, anyway. The only thing outside was the hall and elevator.

Going back into the living room, she thought, "Now that I'm in Lake Tahoe, I'd like to visit a casino, but I don't know how to get there. I'll bet Maddie knows."

She opened the entry doors to call for her guide. She blinked in shock. She was in a casino, complete with blackjack tables, roulette wheels, craps tables, slot machines, and games she'd never seen. She stopped and felt frightened for a moment. Seconds ago, that had been the hallway.

"I get it," she said. "This is what they meant by saying, if you want something ask. I could get used to this."

She was tempted to enter and play, but she decided to clean up and get ready for dinner.

"Now that I know how to reach the casino, I can go whenever I want. I'll give it a try after dinner. No one will miss me tonight."

CHAPTER THIRTEEN

As Kim strolled out of the garden, she almost ran into the young woman who served her the drink.

"Hi. I'm Karen. Can I show you to your campsite?"

"Sure. I'm looking forward to it. It seems strange to go camping without any gear. I'm dying to see what they have rigged up for me."

Karen smiled, "You'll be pleasantly surprised. I'm not much of a camper, but I love your place."

"I need to get my car and Bailey."

"No problem. Both are all settled in at your campsite."

"Bailey went somewhere without me?"

"I think he likes me. Of course, jerky treats helped. He was happy and content when I left him. He's a sweet dog."

"Yes, jerky does it every time."

They left the garden and followed a path heading through the woods. Kim looked back and couldn't see the garden. She couldn't see the castle either. She was surrounded by lush, green forest.

"Things here change so rapidly," she said. How'll I find my way around? We just left the garden, but it's gone. I have no idea where the castle is."

"This may sound strange," Karen explained, "but, you can't get lost around here. Trust me. All you have to do is follow a trail—any trail—and it'll take you where you want to go. I understand you like to hike."

"Yes, but I usually have a trail map or some idea where I'm going. I'm good with directions, like north and south, but nothing here seems to have a direction."

Karen laughed. "You can't get lost. If all else fails, call for me. I'll be there. Just tell a trail where you want to go, and it takes you."

Kim was confused. "You make it sound as if the trails have ears."

Karen nodded. "You may never understand this place. The best advice I can give you is to think of it as a wonderful dream or fantasy. It is governed by imagination, not reality."

Suddenly a clearing opened up, and the women walked into a huge campsite. Kim's car was parked at the edge of the clearing, and Bailey was asleep on his bed outside the door of a tent.

It was one of the biggest tents Kim had seen. She looked at the car and wondered how it got there. There were no roads through the forest. She decided not to ask.

"That's huge," Kim stated. "It looks like a small circus tent. Is it all for me?"

"Sure is, but there's more than meets the eye at this camp. Let me show you around, then you can do what you want until dinner."

Kim looked at her watch. It still showed three o'clock. "It's confusing when time doesn't change. How'll I know when it's time for dinner."

"When you're hungry, head for the castle. That's dinnertime."

Kim sighed, "Okay. Whatever you say. Are we all programmed to get hungry simultaneously? I feel like a little kid."

"You'll do fine if you keep a child's mind and imagination. Relax and enjoy this place. Few women get such an experience. Now, in addition to your tent, you have a picnic table and chairs. There's a fire circle over there, with plenty of firewood."

"Nice. Will I have time to enjoy them?"

"You haven't seen anything yet," Karen added. "In the back is your bathhouse. Go look inside."

Kim was astounded. The bathhouse was as large as an apartment. It looked like a ritzy cabana for a movie. She half-expected to see Esther Williams come hopping out with a towel around her head.

She opened the sliding glass door. Inside was a swimming pool with Jacuzzi. On the other side was an exercise room with all the latest equipment, even a massage table

"I suppose all I have to do is say I want a massage, and someone will give it to me?"

Karen smiled, "Of course. In this room is your tub, shower, toilet—the necessities. This wall moves and behind it is your kitchen and dining area." She demonstrated.

"That's not a kitchen, it's a gourmet's heaven. It has everything." She opened the refrigerator and found it stocked with things she liked.

"If you don't see what you want...."

"I know. Ask for it."

"You've got it. I have to go. Have fun."

When Kim turned around to acknowledge Karen, she was gone.. Kim shook her head. In her wildest dreams she never would've imagined the weekend would turn out like this. She wished Linda could see it, too.

She walked back to the tent. Bailey raised his head and yawned.

"You're probably the only one who understands what's going on, and you can't talk. Although, they said if I wanted anything.... Bailey, tell me what's going on?"

Bailey walked over to her and kissed her cheek as she knelt.

"No? Maybe that's something that's not within reason. I probably would've fainted if you said anything."

She petted his head and noticed someone set out food and water for him. He even had his cow hooves and toys. She went to the car to unpack her things, but it was empty.

"How silly of me," she chuckled. "I'm sure that's been taken care of."

She opened the tent flap and wondered why she kept being surprised at what she found. The tent was larger than her bedroom at home. It had a queen-sized bed, and a nightstand with a lamp on it. She turned it on.

"Right. I'm supposed to believe this tent and the bathhouse are wired for electricity?" She picked up the lamp. There was no cord.

"Batteries? But what about the television set and refrigerator, the Jacuzzi? Maybe I shouldn't think about those."

There was a large, portable closet in the tent, and her clothes were hung neatly inside. Beside it was a chest of drawers and a dresser.

"I know I don't have to look, but I will." She found all her clothes neatly arranged.

She sat on the bed. Bailey leaped up beside her and licked her face. They wrestled for a few minutes. Kim covered him with the bedspread and played Hide and Seek.

"Pretty neat, Bailey. All the comforts of home. Linda would enjoy camping more if it were like this. To think, when I asked for a tent, I hoped it would be big enough for both of us."

She rested with Bailey beside her, then she got up. "We need to find the camera. We have to take picture of this. No one will believe us."

Kim took pictures of the tent, inside and out, pictures of the bathhouse and her car at the campsite. When she started photographing the trees, she said, "Good thing I brought plenty of film. I have a feeling I'm going to use it all."

Bailey went into the bathhouse with her when she decided to shower and prepare for dinner. Out of habit, she looked at her watch. Three o'clock.

"If they aren't worried, why should I?"

Deciding what to wear was the next problem. "They might have something special planned for tomorrow night, so I'll save my better clothes just in case, and wear something more casual tonight."

She opted for her white and lavender running suit. It was comfortable and looked good. She would wear her turtleneck under the jacket in case it turned cold.

Kim laughed, "Cold? Here? Julia probably has her computer regulating the weather with constant temperature."

She chided herself, noting that even Julia couldn't control Mother Nature.

When she was ready, Kim turned to Bailey. "I'm ready for dinner, and I'm hungry, so it must be time. I hope the others are hungry, too. Julia must have programmed us somehow, without our knowing it. Guess I'll head down the trail, or is it up the trail to the castle?"

She was reluctant to leave Bailey by himself in a strange place. "I hate leaving you here. Maybe I should take you with me and tie you outside the castle. You would behave, wouldn't you?"

"Not to worry," came Karen's voice from outside the tent. "He would probably be more comfortable here with his bed and toys. I'll make sure he eats and I'll take him for a walk. He does like me."

Bailey ran over to Karen and kissed her hand.

"Sure, he knows where the treats are," Kim noted.

"He'll be fine. Go and enjoy your dinner."

"That's wonderful, Karen. Thanks. I ordered lobster for dinner, and I sure don't want to miss that. You be good, Bailey."

She headed to the trailhead and winked at Karen. "Let's see. Is this how you do it? Take me to the castle."

She waved and walked away.

CHAPTER FOURTEEN

Kate walked through the woods with her guide. "I'm sorry, I wasn't paying attention when you told me your name."

"Call me Kathy."

"Oh, yes, I remember. It's been a long and confusing day. I look forward to relaxing."

"I'll bet you do. You came the farthest."

They walked on.

"How long have you worked for Julia?"

"You know, that's funny," Kathy chuckled. "I feel like I've worked with her forever. Actually, this is my first assignment with her."

"Really? You seem like old friends."

"She's easy to be with. Everything flows around her. There are never any glitches."

"What's she really like?"

"Without exception, she's the most considerate, nonjudgmental person I ever met. She's in a category all her own."

"Does she pay you well?"

Kathy glared at her.

Kate felt uneasy. "I'm from New York. We always ask how much. Sorry if I intruded."

"That's okay. You caught me by surprise. Let's just say she's paying me more than I could've expected."

"You must work for an agency or something."

"Why?"

"You said this was your first assignment with her."

"Oh, that. I hire myself out for odd jobs all the time. I call them assignments, not jobs. Jobs sounds so permanent. These are temporary."

"You have many assignments like this?"

Kathy laughed, "Hardly. Each one's different."

"Yes, but how can it be fun to be a nursemaid for an African-American attorney?"

"It beats being nursemaid to a Caucasian contractor," she giggled. "Seriously, having the chance to meet you face-to-face is one of the most fun things I've done."

Kate didn't believe it. "You must not have had much fun in your life. What do you know about me?"

"You'd be surprised."

Kate didn't know what to make of Kathy's remarks and she was too tired to pursue it. She would save that for later.

As they rounded a corner, they neared a large motor home nestled between the trees. It looked too big to be on wheels.

"Wow," Kate said. "That's not what I expected."

"Are you disappointed?"

"Hell, no. It's gorgeous. I was expecting a small pickup truck with a shell on top. This is self-contained and bigger than a bus."

She stared at the light-blue motor home with dazzling white trim. There were rows of torches around it. At night, they'd make the vehicle glow.

"How big is it?"

"Julia told me it has eight hundred square feet of living space. That doesn't count the outside extras she ordered for you. She wanted you to be comfortable."

"Comfortable? An entire family could live in it."

"Before we go in, let me show you some of the other things you have. Out back is a deck overlooking the lake, complete with pool and Jacuzzi."

They walked around the motor home.

"Here's your pool house," Kathy continued. "It has a complete bathroom and fully stocked party room. There's a pool table at one end—we know you like the game. If you want anything else for your entertainment, please ask."

"How'd you know I like to shoot pool? I don't tell many people about that."

Kathy shrugged, "We know a lot about you."

"Do you have any idea how frightening that sounds? It's like you can read my mind."

"That would seem frightening, but remember, everything we know about you will never be used against you, or thrown in your face. It's just a part of knowing who you are. We have your best interests at heart. Let's go inside."

"Do you have the keys?"

Kathy smiled. "We don't need keys here, but if you'd feel better with it locked...."

"That's all right. I forget we're not in New York."

"If you need anything...."

"I know. Just ask."

Kate opened the door and walked in. It was immaculately clean and tastefully decorated. She turned to speak to Kathy, but she was gone.

The front room was large enough for Kate to throw a party for her friends. Beautiful blue and mauve drapes adorned the windows. The light-gray carpet looked so lush, she kicked off her shoes and sank peacefully into the soft nap. At one end of the room was a large-screen television and entertainment center, complete with reel-to-reel tapes and a CD player.

Off the front room was a kitchen and dining area. There was a built-in hutch and chandelier hanging over an oak table, which was surrounded by maroon-backed chairs on rollers.

Kate sat in a chair and rolled through the kitchen. It was completely stocked as if they expected her to entertain the conference for dinner.

"Good luck to the others if they want me to cook. Julia knows that's not one of my strengths.

She opened the refrigerator. It was filled with beverages and snacks. "I couldn't eat all that if I lived here a month. Someone must use it when Julia isn't having a conference."

She removed a soda and an apple, set them on the butcher-block counter, and wheeled back to the table.

A small closet in the hallway housed an apartment-sized washer and dryer.

She ventured into the bedroom. It was almost as big as the living room. The same style of drapes hung on the windows and through them was a magnificent view of the lake. A king-sized bed graced the middle of the room. She opened the oak dresser drawers and found her things neatly arranged. A large closet took up one side of the room. Her things were hung in it, but hardly filled one section of one side.

"Maybe I should've brought more," she mused.

The bathroom was large enough for several people to use without crowding. The walls were papered with an Oriental pattern in a modern design. The burgundy floor mats and bath towels accented the curtains and matched perfectly. Everything was built-in, and she spent a lot of time pushing buttons to see where things were.

It was a beautiful home, tastefully done in her favorite colors. She washed her face and brushed her teeth before returning to the bedroom. She saw a clock radio on the nightstand and wondered why it was there. It read three o'clock like her watch. She doubted it could be changed.

On top of the chest of drawers was a television set. She found the remote control and scanned through the channels. Maybe she'd find a news show that would give her the correct time. All she saw were movies, ball games, educational programs and the home shopping channel.

"They don't have the Playboy channel."

On the next click, she saw the Playboy logo.

"I was only kidding!" she shouted.

She left the set tuned to an educational program, went back to the kitchen for her soda and apple, and planned what to wear for dinner.

When she started dressing in her blue flannel pants suit, she saw the drawer on the nightstand was slightly open. She pulled it and found her glasses and the book she'd been reading at home.

She decided she was more tired than she thought, because she had packed her glasses, but didn't remember packing the book. She took it out. Her bookmark was right where she left it. She didn't know why she should be surprised by anything that happened, but she was. Even though she decided she must have packed the book, she knew something was going on at the castle that bridged fantasy and reality.

"Although I think I need to just accept things the way they are here, I'm going to see if I can't figure out what's going on," she said to herself. "There seems to be a reason I'm here—a reason we're all here."

Kate finished dressing and decided it was time to leave for the castle and dinner. "I'm hungry, so it must be time. Wish I could get used to this and have some fun with it."

As she stood outside, admiring her motor home, as they called it, she looked at the surrounding forest. There were no roads into the area and other than the clearing where the home stood, there were no other clearings she could see.

"How could they ever get something so big in here without leaving some kind of trail? There's no tire marks or other indication anything was brought through here."

She started down the trail and glanced back. "There must be a logical explanation."

CHAPTER FIFTEEN

Denise found her guide, Danielle, and asked for directions to the bungalow.

"Come on," Danielle offered. "I'll go with you. It's not far." They walked out of the garden and into the forest.

"Where are you from?" Denise asked.

"I grew up in Chicago."

"Really? So did I. You don't sound like you're from there. Where's your family from, your nationality?"

"My mom was Spanish, and my dad was from Puerto Rico."

Denise nodded. "That explains why we look so much alike. That's my ancestry, too. You look a lot like I did when I was younger, including not being so round. Does Julia do this on purpose?"

"Do what?"

"Come on, Danielle, I'm not blind. All of our guides look like us and have the same ethnic background."

"Julia thought it would be more comfortable for you."

Denise considered her explanation. "I guess it makes it easier in a weekend that doesn't make sense anyway. How long have you been in Tahoe? Did you move here from Chicago?"

"This is my first trip to Tahoe. Between Chicago and here, I knocked around awhile."

"Ever live in Texas?"

"Yeah."

"Why am I not surprised?"

"What do you mean?"

"I'm not sure, but it feels like Julia has had our guides spying on us a long while."

"Spying?"

"Yes. You know too much about us. It isn't normal and I don't believe it all came from a computer. How long have you worked for Julia?"

"Denise, you're too suspicious. Why would I spy on you?"

"Because it's part of your job. Maybe...oh, I don't know. It's weird."

"For your information, this is the first time I ever worked for Julia, and I haven't been here much longer than you."

"See? The way you answer questions sounds strange. This is the first time you've worked for Julia, like maybe you knew her before, or you're part of her network. How'd you get the job?"

"I was asked to do it, just like you were asked to come."

"You were chosen by computer? What kind of work do you really do?"

Danielle motioned, "Come on. Don't you want to see your bungalow?"

Before Denise could answer, she saw a clearing. There was a path leading to a bungalow tucked among the trees. They came to a white picket fence, and Danielle opened the gate.

"This is too cute!" Denise exclaimed.

It was the first time she'd seen a log cabin. It was trimmed with white shutters and had white sash windows.

"This is darling."

"You like it?"

"I love it—the fence, the cute path.... Does it go all the way around?"

"Take a look."

They followed the path around the house. It ended in a backyard, where Denise had a beautiful view of the lake. There was a large manicured lawn that sloped to the water, and a boathouse and dock were reflected in the lake.

"Is there a boat in there?" Denise asked.

"There is if you want one."

Denise looked at Danielle, who shrugged.

"Let's go inside," Denise suggested. "I want to see what it's like."

Danielle opened the door.

"It's not locked?"

"You don't need locks around here. No one can get onto the grounds. You're safe."

"Who lives here?"

"Pardon me?"

"Who lives here? Someone has to. You didn't build this bungalow just for me."

"Actually, I don't know.

"Something you don't know? That's a first."

Denise was thrilled with the bungalow. It was decorated in a southwest Native American motif, from the curtains and throw rugs on the hardwood floors, to the artwork hung on the walls.

The living room wasn't large, but it was cozy. At one end of the room was a huge stone fireplace with a fire already burning in it.

"Great fireplace. I don't see any wood."

"It's computer controlled. Everything is. Temperatures are constant and comfortable."

"How do I change it?"

"Tell the computer, and it'll adjust itself."

Denise tried the couch. "This is lovely. At first, I thought these were Native American blankets on the couch, but it's the upholstery. It's soft and warm like blankets."

"I need to be going," Danielle announced. "You should find everything you need. If not, ask."

After Danielle left, Denise began exploring. The kitchen looked like an old country kitchen with Native American designs, almost like grandma's kitchen, but with modern appliances.

"I love these towels," Denise said. "Wonder where I can find some like them?"

There was a laundry room off the kitchen, and she frowned. She hoped she brought enough clothing to avoid doing laundry. She opened the pantry door. It was completely stocked.

When she walked into the bedroom, Denise knew she was in love with the bungalow. The room was much larger than her bedroom. Under a window was a king-sized, four-poster brass bed, just like the one she recently saw in a magazine. The ruffles around the canopy matched the curtains on the windows.

"I always wanted a bed like this." She bounced on the bed like a child.

The dresser looked like an antique, yet it seemed new. Maybe it had been refurbished. She opened drawers and found her things neatly placed in the same way she would have. Instead of a closet, she had an armoire that ran the length of the room along the wall.

Denise ran her fingers over the armoire. It was exquisitely crafted. She never saw a more perfect piece anywhere. She opened the doors and found her clothes hanging inside.

She returned to the kitchen and opened the refrigerator. There was a bottle of her favorite Chardonnay chilling, as if waiting just for her. She opened it and poured a glass. It tasted wonderful.

Denise returned to the bedroom to relax before getting ready for dinner. She found the remote control for the television set which was hanging on the wall. She turned it on and ignored it. She liked the noise.

The decorations in the bathroom complemented those in the rest of the house. The tub had little claw feet like the ones she saw in old pictures, and it was equipped with a Jacuzzi. She toyed with the idea of soaking before dinner, but feared she'd want to sleep afterward.

She walked into the living room and stood by the fire, sipping her wine. She felt safe and secure, without a care, but she couldn't escape the feeling that something strange, almost otherworldly, was going on.

She wanted to talk to Gene, but he had no sense of anything unless it was worldly. Maybe she could talk to the others at dinner and see if they felt the same way. Perhaps not Marge, who seemed to be in her own world.

"Kate and I think alike. Maybe we can get together and chat," Denise said to herself.

She finished her glass of wine and took a shower.

As she dressed for dinner, Denise found herself talking out loud.

"I'm hungry, so it must be time for dinner. Wonder what they are going to do when they discover I'm always hungry?"

CHAPTER SIXTEEN

Kim strolled into the castle lobby just as the other women emerged from their quarters.

"Whew," she sighed. "I'm not the last one to arrive."

The others seemed relieved that the time problem had been resolved.

"Nice we could all meet for dinner at three," Marge stated. "That is what everyone's watch says, isn't it?"

They laughed, glad the tension was broken. They also confirmed the readings on their watches.

"It'll probably be like this until we leave on Sunday," Denise stated. "We'll have to get used to it."

"I'm not sure I like that," Marge complained. "There must be a way to find out what time it is. I'm used to operating on a clock. How the hell did they know we'd all arrive together? How do we know it's dinnertime? It might be over, or not ready for another hour. Must be tough on the cook."

"I kind of liked not being rushed," Kate admitted. "Of course, they knew we'd all be here at the same time. We're here at three."

Marge waved her finger at Kate. "Maybe you think this is fun and games, but we shouldn't take this lightly. There's something very unnatural about this place."

"Really?" Denise teased. "What was your first clue?"

"Yeah," Kim added. "We've known all along this wouldn't be a typical weekend. We had to know something was strange from the beginning, so why not have fun with it? Besides, what else can we do?"

Julia appeared in the doorway to the main dining room. "Good. You're all here. Why don't we sit down for dinner?"

The dining room was large enough to seat one hundred people, but there was one small table set in the middle of the room. It looked minuscule compared to the rest of the trappings. The wallpaper, chandeliers, drapes, and furniture were lavish and elegant.

Their table was set simply. It was a round oak table covered with a checked tablecloth of green so dark it was almost black, mixed with light gray. A small bouquet of roses adorned the center.

"Notice how everything around here is round?" Marge whispered. "I even have a round bed."

The others eyed her.

"That's so we can see what each other is up to," Kate nudged her.

"Yeah, and Julia can spy on all of us at the same time," Denise added.

"Sit anyplace you'd like," Julia instructed. "Dinner is about ready."

After everyone sat, she added, "I assume you're comfortable and have settled in. Are your accommodations adequate?"

"More than adequate," Denise chuckled. "I don't know about the others, but I asked for a bungalow cabin. I didn't expect a first-class resort. I could stay a month. It has everything."

"Oh, big deal," Marge said. "I've got a penthouse suite, complete with a casino."

Kim and Denise raised their eyebrows.

"I never would have guessed Marge would select the penthouse, would you?" Kim asked.

Denise shook her head.

Kate squinted as if thinking hard. "That's interesting. I have completely different accommodations. I asked for the motor home, and I feel like they gave me the Taj Mahal. It's huge and more tastefully furnished than anything I've lived in."

"What do you have, Kim? It doesn't sound like there's much left," Denise noted.

"I have a tent."

"You chose a tent?" Marge exploded. "They gave you all those wonderful choices, and you took a tent? How is it, or do you wish you had something else?"

Kim smiled, "I use the word tent loosely. If you mean something made from canvas, then I have a tent, but it's gigantic. We could all live in it. I also have a pool, pool house, workout room, kitchen and bathroom."

"You have a pool?" Marge asked. "I'm in the penthouse. I should have a pool, too."

Julia grinned, "You do, Marge. Obviously, you didn't go out on the balcony."

"Sure I did. I didn't see a pool. Besides, how could there be a pool off the balcony that high up?"

"Use your imagination. If you really want a pool, check out the balcony when you get back."

"How can you be that high up in a building that's only three stories tall?" Kim asked. "You're the contractor. Explain that."

"I can't. I'm telling you, this place is eerie. I looked out my front door to see if there were any other doors in the hall, then I shut the door and said I wanted to visit a casino. I opened the door to find my guide, and presto, I'm in a casino. I can't explain any of it."

"Ladies," Julia announced, "our salads are being served. If you'd like anything else, please feel free to order."

The women began eating, each deep in thought about what the others had said.

As the table was being cleared, Denise asked, "Has anyone

noticed all our guides are just like us?"

The women nodded.

"I did," Marge said. "Mine's even good-looking like me."

Denise choked.

The main entrees were prepared perfectly, although Denise admitted, with all the excitement, she forgot what she ordered. They were hungry and ate quickly and quietly.

"It's wonderful to see women with healthy appetites," Julia said. "When I was young, people said a woman with a healthy appetite had a clear conscience."

Denise laughed, "Then my conscience must pure. I have the healthiest appetite here. I didn't get to be this size by dieting."

The others chuckled.

"How much do you weigh?" Marge asked.

"None of your business," Denise snapped.

"Don't take it personally. I was just curious. You must have a desk job."

"I don't build barns or pigsties or whatever it is you do."

"Look, I don't build barns. Just because I'm from North Dakota doesn't make me a hayseed. I build custom homes," she said proudly.

"How'd you get started in that?" Kim asked.

"I'm not sure. My daddy was a builder, and I met my first husband on a construction job. Somewhere along the line, I decided I was better at it than most men, and started my own business."

"How many husbands have you had?"

"Three legal ones. So what?"

"Nothing. Like you, I'm just curious. "Do you intend to keep trying until you get it right?"

Marge was irritated. "There are good reasons why my marriages didn't work out."

"Like cheating on your husbands?" Denise queried.

"That's not fair. You wouldn't have known about that if Julia hadn't mouthed off. What about you, Kate? You have a husband?"

She shrugged, "Sure. I've been married to the same man for twenty-three years."

"What's he do?" Denise asked.

"He's an attorney, too. He works in a different firm and specializes in criminal law."

"Must be boring," Marge said.

"Not really. He's a good man, although we have been separated for a few months. We'll probably get back together soon."

"What'd he do, cheat on you?" Marge asked.

"No. He made a mistake in trying to defend someone I was prosecuting, but we solved that."

"What kind of law do you practice?" Kim cut in.

"I deal mostly in accident cases."

Marge roared with laughter. "An ambulance chaser!"

"Good grief, Marge." Kate mumbled, trying to curb her temper.

"Are you happy?" Denise wanted to know.

Kate wasn't certain she wanted to answer. She hadn't taken time recently to consider her happiness. She changed the subject.

"What made you decide to become a CPA?"

"She probably couldn't balance her checkbook, so she decided to work on other people's," Marge joked.

"My God, Marge, you're cynical," Denise criticized. "I'm great at math. I loved it in high school. Since there weren't many female CPAs when I went to college, I thought it was a good place to find a man."

"Did you find one?" Kim asked.

Denise was quiet. She hadn't meant to admit so much. "Sort of. We were engaged, then...he was killed."

"I'm sorry. How'd it happen?"

"Viet Nam," she lied.

"Damn. I hate hearing that. We lost a lot of good men over there. We never should have been involved," Kate stated.

"What do you mean?" Marge asked. "We were there defending our country and saving the world from the spread of communism."

"Oh, please," Kate groaned. "I never fell for that line. I'm surprised you did."

Kim spoke quickly, "So, you never married after that?"

"No. I wasn't interested in another man until recently."

"Now there's someone?"

"I don't know. I've been dating a nice man. We'll wait and see."

"What about you, Kim?" Kate asked. "Are you married?"

"Not exactly."

"What's that supposed to mean?" Marge interrupted. "Either you are or you aren't."

"I'm not married."

"Maybe she lives with him, Marge," Denise said. "You don't have to get married, you know."

Kim didn't answer.

Marge looked at her. "Is that it? Do you live with a guy?"

"I have a partner."

"What's he like?" Denise pushed.

Kim was hoping they'd drop it, but they weren't. She didn't care what they thought, and she was certain Julia already knew.

"My partner's a woman."

"You're queer?" Marge shouted.

Kim stood.

"Jesus, Marge!" Kate yelled. "You're tactless and rude!"

"I'm not queer, Marge," Kim responded quietly. "I have a woman for a partner and I'm very happy in the relationship."

"Christ, why a woman? What can she possibly do for you that a man can't?" Marge demanded.

"She does more for me than all your men have been able to do for you." Kim sat down.

Denise laughed, "Yeah, Marge. Maybe you should consider women. It might work better."

Kate waved her hand and tried to catch her breath. "God, no. Don't do that to another woman. It's bad enough if she drives men crazy. Can you imagine trying to live with her?"

Marge was indignant. "What's that supposed to mean? I'm sure there are plenty of gay women who'd love to live with me. Do you think it's hard to get along with me?"

"I wouldn't touch that with a ten-foot pole," Kate said. "It would be like handing your sister a lit stick of dynamite."

"I don't see anything wrong with being gay," Denise said. "As long as you're happy and not hurting anyone, it's fine. How long have you and your partner been together, and what's her name?"

"Linda. We've been together fifteen years."

"I hate to interrupt in the middle of getting to know one another," Julia spoke, "but we've some business to attend to. As soon as you finish your desserts, we'll get started. We have some delicious chocolate mousse to finish off our meals."

"What?" Marge asked. "We can't order what we want?"

"You could, but I'd like to get the first session started. In the interest of time, I have expedited matters."

"She probably knows we all like it, too," Denise added.

CHAPTER SEVENTEEN

After the table was cleared, and everyone sat back to relax, Julia stood.

"Ladies, please continue with your coffee while I outline plans for the weekend. Now that you're settled in, if you wish to talk to each other, you'll find a telephone directory in your quarters that explains how to reach each other. If you have any difficulties, call your personal guide. Do you have any questions?"

Marge raised her hand. "I have one about my guide. Will she know everything I do?"

Julia laughed, "Basically, yes."

"Does she report to you or someone about me? I don't know the rules here, and I don't want to get into trouble."

"Heavens, Dear. No one reports on you. No one cares what you do. This conference is for you. I did not make any rules. Whatever happens is between you and your guide. Perhaps you don't truly understand who they are."

"Who are they?" Denise asked.

"Think of them as extensions of yourselves."

"See? I was right, they're just like us," Marge gloated.

"That's true. Anything you share with your guide will be confidential."

"They sound more like guardian angels," Denise pointed out.

Julia smiled, "Yes, they are."

"Can we take them with us when we leave?" Kim asked.

"Good question," Kate chipped in.

"Not physically," Julia replied, "but, they've been with you all your lives in many ways, and they'll continue with you on the rest of your journey."

"What do you mean, they've been with us?" Kate questioned.

"You've never been aware of them until now. Get to know them, and you'll see they're more like you than you can imagine."

"Do they have the same problems and faults?" Marge asked.

"Come on, Marge," Kate said. "No one could have that many problems and faults."

"Cute."

"Consider your guides as perfect. They do not have your problems or faults. You'd do well to learn from them. They're willing to help."

All four nodded, but each woman struggled within as confusion continued to grow.

"The first thing I want you to do this evening, is go to your offices," Julia continued. "Fix them up however you please. Equip them with whatever you want. Make them comfortable, but functional. I'd like you to work there. Outside your office, you're on your own. Have fun."

"What kind of work are you expecting?" Kim asked.

"Here's what I'm hoping for. I want to see you come up with a plan or format other women can follow when they turn fifty. The four of you are so different, I assume there will be four plans. Hopefully, they'll be something that announces to women and the public that she has turned fifty, and that it's a positive move. I want the plans to help each woman take a positive view of her future and who she is."

"That's a tall order," Kate said.

"What makes you think we're the ones who can do this? Asking all four of us to speak for all women is a bit presumptuous," Denise added.

"You won't be setting down a formula cast in stone. You'll set guidelines for others to follow, adjust, and change to suit their needs. You'll give them permission to push on in a positive, viable way."

"Still," Marge cut in, "how many women would be interested in my ideas?"

"You'd be surprised."

"In other words," Kim started slowly, "we're trying to improve women's image of themselves and to develop self-esteem to help them through the fifties menopause crisis."

"Jesus," Marge cried. "Are you going through menopause?"

"Not yet. Are you?"

"Hell, no. I won't be fifty until July thirty-first."

"Really?" Denise asked. "That's my birthday."

"Mine, too," Kim added.

All eyes turned to Kate.

"Why should I be different? It's my birthday, too," Kate said.

They stared at Julia.

"Well, that didn't take long to surface. See how fast you're progressing? I didn't think you'd figure that out until sometime tomorrow."

"What gives?" Marge asked.

Julia sighed, "I might as well let the rest of it out. What time were you born, Kim?"

"Nine forty-five."

"Morning or evening?"

"Morning."

"That doesn't jive with me," Marge said. "I was born at ten

forty-five in the morning."

"In what state?" Denise pressed.

"Montana."

"Kim?"

"California."

"Bingo!" Denise threw up her arms. "Same time, Marge, different time zone. I was born at eleven forty-five in Chicago, so I assume Kate was born...."

"At twelve forty-five in New York," she confirmed.

Marge's eyes widened. "You mean we were born on the same date and time fifty years ago? What are the odds on that?"

"We don't want to know, do we, Julia?" Kate questioned.

The elderly woman smiled silently.

Denise stood, "Come on, Julia, make it complete. Tell us you were born on July thirty-first, 1895 at...."

"Nine forty-five in the morning in California," Julia stated.

Kate felt anxious. "This is spooky. Not only the odds of such a thing happening and our all still being alive, but your finding us, are astronomical. How the hell did you do it?"

"It took a while," Julia admitted. "Our computer did quite a job, wouldn't you say?"

"So there was a lot more to your computer search than you told us?" Kim pushed.

Julia bowed her head.

The women were silent. Marge muttered something about needing a glass of water. It was immediately brought to her. She downed it. The others were stunned, unsure what to do next.

"What time is it?" Kate looked at her watch.

"Good question," Julia jumped in. "It's time to get started with your work areas and assignments."

"How long are we supposed to work on this tonight?" Kim asked.

"As long as you like. Our next meeting will be here in the morning for breakfast. I'd like you to have a short work session after we eat. Then, the rest of the day will be yours."

Julia stood and left the women. The four women stared after her.

"I wonder what other revelations we'll have about each other this weekend?" Denise asked.

"You can bet there will be more," Kate observed. "I'm not going to be surprised by anything else that happens while we're here. We have not seen the end of this."

"Maybe we ought to share our personal stuff now," Marge suggested, "so there won't be any surprises later."

"Easy for you to say. We know about you, your three husbands, and your boyfriend," Kate said. "Maybe the rest of us don't want to share."

"Come on. What can be so dark in your lives? We know Kim's gay, Denise has a boyfriend, and you and your husband are separated."

"Now we know what she meant by we were all going through some personal problems," Kate added.

Denise turned to Kim. "I'll bet your family doesn't take too well to your being gay."

"That's an understatement." Kim explained the problems she had with her family and with being a schoolteacher.

Kate opened up and told her story about the lawsuit she won and how Ronald had backed out of the case, after she threw him out of the house.

Denise finally broke down and told the others the truth about Derrick dying in her arms during the shootout, and how she was wounded, too.

"So, now we know about each other's struggles," Kate stated.

"She got four good ones on that," Marge added.

"There must be some more coincidences about us that we don't know yet," Denise observed. "If we continue to talk and communicate with each other, they are bound to come out."

"I'm sure Julia has a plan. We'll never figure it on our own," Kim said.

"You're right," Kate agreed. "Let's get started on our assignments. This might turn out better than we expect. Let the surprises fall where they may."

CHAPTER EIGHTEEN

Kate left the dining room, waved to the others, and opened her office door.

"Let's see," she said. "What do I need? I want a wall mural with the New York skyline on it."

She turned and saw the mural on the opposite wall.

"Great. This is fun." She added paintings and a mirror on the other walls.

"I need something to sit in while I finish furnishing this room. How about a nice leather chair with matching sofa, a large oak desk, and two lamps?"

Two women walked in carrying furniture. She sat in the chair behind the desk and thought.

"I need a work table, computer, telephone, and fax machine."

Once those were in place, Kate sent faxes to everyone in New York she knew. The messages were the same—she was at Lake Tahoe in a beautiful magical castle where she could have anything she wanted. She never noticed that none of the faxes were delivered.

Now all she had to do was develop a rite of passage.

*   *   *   *

The first thing Marge did in her office was ask for a wet bar. When she opened the louvered closet doors, she found the bar, complete with a refrigerator. She popped open a cold Michelob and asked for a desk and chair so she could sit and enjoy her beer. Thinking the room was a little bare, she ordered a telephone, large-screen TV, a lamp, and a Nintendo game.

Marge leaned back in the chair and rested her feet on the desk. She turned on the TV and found an old movie.

"This is great, an Annette and Frankie beach-party movie. God, they must be fifty by now. I wonder how they'll celebrate? Maybe with a beach party."

She fumbled with her pockets. "I thought I had some cigarettes." She frowned. "Maddie, I know you're out there. Where are my damn cigarettes?"

Maddie opened the door. "Sorry, Julia doesn't allow smoking in the castle."

"I should've known. Good, old, pure Julia. I don't plan to live to be one hundred. What does she do for fun?"

Maddie shrugged, "Beats the hell out of me."

"Got any cigarettes?"

"Follow me."

They went outside, away from the castle. The night air was cool. The sky was clear, and stars shone brightly. Maddie took out two cigarettes, lit them, and handed one to Marge.

"I didn't know you smoked, Maddie."

"I'm an extension of you, remember? If you don't live to be one hundred, I won't either."

Marge looked at her guide carefully. "What do you do when you're not guiding a contractor from North Dakota around a castle?"

"Are you sure you want to know?"

"Of course."

"I'm always trying to guide a contractor from North Dakota. I have to admit, I enjoy the change of scenery."

"Come on. You don't expect me to believe your job in life is to be my guardian angel."

"No, I'd never expect you to believe."

"Then what gives?"

Maddie grinned. "All I can say is, I'm always around and have been since you can remember. That probably goes back.... Let's see. The first thing you remember in life was Buffy."

Marge's jaw dropped. "Buffy was my first imaginary friend when I was two. How could you know about her? I never even told Mom what her name was."

"You came up with Buffy shortly after your father left." Maddie scrunched her lips.

"Christ, I used to do that with my lips when I was a kid." Marge was silent, then laughed. "I get it. Now you want me to believe you were Buffy."

"Believe what you want. I was glad when you changed my name to Sunny."

"I only did that so no one would know if my friend was a boy or girl."

"We both know you spelled it S-U-N-N-Y."

Marge extinguished her cigarette in the ashtray Maddie suddenly produced.

"Play with my mind all you want. I'm not buying any of it."

"I know."

Marge returned to her office alone. The beach -party movie was still on.

"That's it. The way to celebrate one's rite of passage is to throw a party."

She ran to her desk. "There must be paper and pencils in here." She opened drawers, found what she needed, and started writing ideas for a party.

"Julia will probably want more than just having an idea for a party. She'll want details. Let's see. I can plan this for myself. I could rent the Veteran's Hall in Minot. That's good. Maybe I could borrow Julia's printer and have some gold-embossed invitations printed. Hell, why stop there? I'll have flyers put up all over town."

She sat on the floor in front of the television, propping her head against the back of the desk.

"This is fun. Should I have people bring gifts? Of course. Hell, I want lots of gifts, but it's too tacky to ask people to bring them. I could tell a few friends that if anyone asked, tell them to bring a gift. I like it."

Marge smiled, "Julia must think I'll be the last one to come up with an idea, if she thinks I'll get one at all."

She stood as if ready to make an announcement. "No, I'm not done yet. I'll hire a band to play some good, old-fashioned county music. I know the band, too. We'll have a fully stocked bar and some catered food—nothing fancy."

Then she had a thought.

"How the hell will I pay for all that? I'll ask people to pay for their drinks. We could sell them cheap. The food and music would be free. The way my friends drink, I could make enough money to pay for the whole bash, and I'd have all those presents, too. I could go to different stores in town and put my name on things, just like registering for a wedding."

Maddie stuck her head in the door. "That last part's a bit tacky, even for you."

"Is nothing sacred?"

Still, Maddie was right. Marge crossed out the last part of her plan.

"The party should last all night."

She went to her desk, asked for a calendar, and found one in a drawer.

132

"Wouldn't you know, the thirty-first is a Monday? That's a bad party night. You'd think Julia could've planned better. We'll have the party on Saturday, the twenty-ninth. That was the day Mom thought I'd be born. If I had been, I wouldn't be here now."

She folded the paper and stuck it in a drawer. "I don't want to do too much in my first session. They'd expect too much of me. Besides, I want to try that casino."

She turned out the lights, closed the door, and took the elevator to her suite.

* * * *

When Denise entered her office, she immediately began requesting items.

"I want a desk and a large, comfortable chair, two floor lamps and a wastebasket."

Once those were in place, she added a work table, adding machine, calculator, computer, and copy machine. The items arrived promptly.

"Too bad this is for the weekend. I could get used to this. It would be nice to have some music in here." She looked toward the ceiling. "Would it be too much to ask for a CD player?"

Danielle opened the door, "You requested music, oh Rotund One?"

"Only you can get away with that," Denise responded.

Danielle held the door open as two women brought in a complete entertainment center. As soon as it was set up, Danielle started pushing buttons.

"Oh, Trini Lopez. My favorite. How'd you know?"

"I just do."

Denise grew serious. "Is there anything you don't know about me?"

"Only the things you don't know, either."

*   *   *   *

Kim was tired. She wanted to head back to her campsite and Bailey, but she felt obligated to start on her assignment.

She walked into the empty office and thought how drab it looked. She wanted windows and a view. She spun around and found a huge picture window taking up most of one wall.

"I'll need drapes. Perhaps something blue."

Two women came in and started hanging drapes.

"This is easy. I'll need a desk and chair. I could also use a typewriter, paper, pencils, stapler, and all that normal office stuff. I don't know why, but I feel naked without a blackboard. I might as well have a lamp, too. Oh, yes—a telephone and a computer."

She looked around as the items were delivered. "Why do I need all these things?"

Karen popped her head in the room, "You expect me to answer that?"

"Oh, Karen. Come in, please. I could use some help."

"Wait. You need another chair." Karen motioned and an overstuffed chair was brought. "See? I can do it too." She sat down and threw her legs over the arm.

"Karen, I'm a bit overwhelmed by all this. I don't know what I expected, but, somehow, I don't feel like I fit in."

"In what way?"

"I'm the only gay woman here, and my tastes don't seem as, well, grandiose as the others. You know. I'm in a tent, while they've got penthouses and everything."

"Are you unhappy with your accommodations?"

"Not at all. It's perfect for me. I just don't think I have much in common with the others. They're nice enough, but they're not like me."

Karen leaned back in her chair. "Did you ever stop to think maybe that's why you're here? Maybe Julia didn't want carbon-copy women. The others probably feel the same way because none of you are the same. Don't you feel you have a lot ot offer this conference?"

"I don't know, maybe."

"There are a lot of lesbians out there, not all of them open about it. Perhaps you can help them. They age, too. They have to deal with menopause, and have partners who deal with it. They have problems with their families. Maybe the issues are a little different for them, but they still face the same things all women face."

Kim shrugged, "I know, but I don't think I can help. Until this conference, I didn't even think about turning fifty. I haven't started menopause."

"Linda has."

"You know about that?"

"Oh, please. Give me some credit. Anyway, how has that been for you?"

Kim laughed. "It sure doesn't make me look forward to it—hot flashes, mood changes, and the physical and emotional swings. It makes dealing with problems and each other more difficult. I'm not excited about it."

"What bothers you the most?"

"Dealing with my family. I can't handle them now. Imagine when I'm menopausal."

Karen nodded, "Families can be a hassle."

"My mother and I haven't spoken in years, because she's unhappy I'm gay. My sister tells me they don't even think of me as family. Mom's upset because I don't have children, and soon, I won't be able to. She'll consider me worthless."

"Did you ever want children?"

"Not really."

Karen sat up. "You're in a tough situation. It looks as if part of your rite of passage has to somehow include your family. They need to know you're a real person, a viable woman with much to offer them and others. Incorporating your family into your passage will be a special challenge."

"Thanks. That's what I needed to hear. The impossible dream still lies ahead. I guess I do need to be here to figure things out."

Karen smiled, "That's what we're trying to do on this planet—figure things out." She stood.

"You're not going, are you?"

"Don't you have things to do?"

"I suppose, but I'm too tired, and I enjoy talking to you."

"Why? Because I'm Japanese and a lesbian?"

"No," Kim answered, "because you seem so much like me. I feel like we've met and talked before."

Karen beamed, "We have, many times."

"We have?"

"Trust me. You'll figure it out. Come on, I'll walk back to camp with you. You don't look like you'll get much more done tonight."

They left the office and walked down the trail. As they passed, lights came on automatically, luminating the trail ahead and showing the way.

"Julia thinks of everything, doesn't she?" Kim chuckled.

"As far as I can tell, she hasn't missed a thing."

"How long have you worked for her?"

Karen stopped and looked at Kim. "I don't work for Julia."

"You don't? Then who do you work for?"

"I thought you knew. I work for you."

Kim was confused, "What do you mean?"

"Think about it. I'm never off with Julia or meeting with her. She doesn't tell me what to do. I'm only here for you, whenever you need me. You're my only concern."

"Sure, but who pays you?"

"I'm one of the fortunate ones whose job is paid in dividends, not cash."

"What a crock. You have to be paid."

"My rewards come from guiding you through life, helping you, seeing you succeed and be happy. That's all the payment I need."

"You make it sound like you're nothing but a guardian angel."

"Nothing but a guardian angel? What a put-down. That's one of the most important jobs anyone could have. Then, to have the opportunity to come face-to-face with you...."

"Why are you telling me this?"

"I thought you could handle it."

Kim sighed, "I don't know how to tell you this, but I don't believe in guardian angels."

"That's why we prefer to be called personal guides."

"It's the same thing. You sound like a real person, but you don't have an identity. Is being my guide all you've ever done?"

"You could say that. Is being you all you've ever done?"

"Touche. If you've been there all along, why haven't we met before?"

"We have, many times. Think about it. Who were you writing to in your diary? Who talked you out of stealing that candy bar

137

when you were six?"

"Wait. I wrote that diary to myself."

"Who was it who told you to follow your heart when you thought you were gay? Who was it that kept you from lying about...."

"Hold it. All those things, well, I was just talking to myself."

"And you think there was no one who listened, supported, and kept you on the right track?"

"But, all that comes from within me. I have a conscience, you know."

"Voila!"

CHAPTER NINETEEN

Kate closed the door to her office and looked around. "Kathy, are you here?"

"Right behind you. What's up?"

"I don't know. I'm at a loss. I thought maybe you'd walk me back to my place."

"How are you feeling lost?"

"More ways than I want to think about." Kate looked at the dark trail and said, "You must have a flashlight. Julia wouldn't leave you in the dark."

Kathy motioned to Kate, and they started down the trail. Lights came on ahead to show the way. "You're right, Julia wouldn't leave us in total darkness."

As they walked, Kate said, "That's it. I feel like I'm in total darkness. How am I supposed to help other women turning fifty when I'm not sure how to do it myself?"

"You don't know how to turn fifty?"

"So many things are up in the air for me. I have just realized I'll never have children. I never thought about it before, because my career was more important. Now, it's too late.

"I'm not sure what to do about Ronald, either. I love him, but I can't let go of my anger. If I go back to him, will I ever trust him again? And, if I don't go back to him, what will I do? I'm not even sure I want to continue practicing law. Does that sound like a fifty-year-old who's together enough to help other women?"

Kathy nodded. "You bet. You will resolve your issues, and in so doing, you'll find new inner strength and being. That'll make you more of a help to others."

"Does Julia pay you extra for these little pep talks?"

"Of course not."

"Another thing I don't understand is how you can always be available. How do you know I need you? Don't you ever take a break?"

"Kate, you have more important issues to deal with than what I do with my time. You must be tired. Go on ahead and get some rest."

"I will, but I intend to figure this place out. I don't know how, but I will. Things aren't what they seem. I won't let it rest." She waved good-bye and continued on her way.

Once inside her motor home, Kate took out her address book. "I need to talk to some people. I'll call my friends. They can do some searching for me and maybe find out something about Julia. A couple of them might even have an idea for a rite of passage. Julia won't mind if I pool ideas."

She called her best friend Martha and got the answering machine.

"Martha, this is important. Get back to me as soon as possible. I'm at Lake Tahoe. We're doing a conference to develop a rite of passage for women turning fifty. What are you going to do to celebrate? Call some of our friends and ask them, too. You can fax me at...."

She wanted to give Martha the number, but realized she didn't know it. "Kathy, what's the fax number here?"

"I think it's 555-50-1995."

"Thanks. Martha, the number is...." She heard the machine click off.

"Damn."

Kathy walked in. "I hate to rain on your parade, but Julia said you wouldn't be able to tell anyone why you're here."

"I can't? Well, maybe a fax can. I'll send a message."

"It won't be received."

"We'll see about that. Why don't you go back to the castle? I won't need you. See you tomorrow."

"Okay, but don't be disappointed if you don't get any responses." Kathy closed the door.

"That's it," Kate said. "Julia can block incoming messages. Maybe the information can get out and someone can start working on this."

She sent a fax to her investigator, asking him to find out about Julia Worthington, born July 31, 1895 in California. He should check telephone records for the castle and find out who owned it. She spent hours sending faxes to friends. Finally, tired and exhausted, she crawled into bed.

*   *   *   *

Denise left her office without thinking about doing any work. She was tired and wanted to ponder the day's events by herself, in her bungalow. She gasped when she walked in the door. She had forgotten how beautiful it was.

"I wish I could take this home with me, but it would look strange on my street in Dallas."

She poured a glass of wine and curled up on the couch in front of the fire.

She wondered how she was supposed to think of something for other women when she didn't know what to do for herself. Maybe Julia had a therapist she could see.

She decided to call Gene. She looked at her watch and made a face. She had no idea what time it was in Texas. When Gene's answering machine came on, Denise couldn't remember if this was his weekend to be in Houston or not.

"Hi, Gene. It's Denise. I'm all settled here. What a beautiful place. You should see the charming bungalow I have. I don't have to share it with anyone, either. I have to admit, I wouldn't mind sharing it with you. I'm enjoying a terrific California Chardonnay. Maybe I can bring back a bottle. You'll love it.

"I'm still not sure what I'm doing here. There are only four of us and we're supposed to come up with a rite of passage...."

The machine clicked off.

"Damn that machine. It always does that."

She hung up, turned on the television, and fell asleep on the couch watching a program about California bears.

*   *   *   *

Marge walked past rows of slot machines and people, smiling and nodding as if she knew them. She liked the fast-paced action.

A cocktail waitress walked up. "Care for anything, Marge?"

"You know me?"

"Of course. You're a special guest at the castle's Fantasy Casino."

"That's the name of this place?"

The waitress nodded.

"I'll have a Black Russian."

Once she had her drink, Marge stopped at a blackjack table. "I might as well try my luck."

She chose a table with three younger men. "How's the dealer?"

"She's been hot." One man pointed to an empty chair. "Why don't you take a seat and change her luck?"

142

Marge sat and bought in with fifty dollars. She played for more than an hour, ordering several drinks, before she noticed she was winning.

The man beside her eyed her stack of chips. "Looks like you're doing well."

Marge was amazed. "Yeah, how about that? I haven't been paying much attention. That must be how it works."

"Where are you from?"

"North Dakota. You?"

"I live here in Tahoe."

"What's your name?"

"Frank Delano."

"Nice to meet you," she smiled. "I'm Marge."

They played for hours, exchanging personal information about each other. They discussed what they did for a living, and each lied about being married.

Finally, Frank said, "Since we seem hell-bent on gambling all night, maybe we can have breakfast together in a few hours. What do you say?"

Marge almost accepted. "I can't. Frank. I already have plans. Maybe we could get together later. I'm here for a conference, and...."

She woke in her room and didn't remember how she got there. She had a gigantic headache, too.

"I don't remember coming back here. I was talking to Frank. We were going out later."

Marge walked into the kitchen to make coffee. "It's just as well I didn't stay any longer. I have to meet the others for breakfast. Hope I didn't oversleep."

CHAPTER TWENTY

Julia addressed the women at Saturday's breakfast. "Good to see you all here bright and early. I hope you slept well. Have a good time last night, Marge?"

Marge still had a hangover and had no idea how she had made it on time. "Is nothing sacred around here?"

"I'm not judging you. I merely wanted to know if you had a good time."

Marge nodded sheepishly.

Julia continued, "The plan for today is simple. You can do whatever you like. I hope you'll spend time on your rite of passage, but that can be done whenever and wherever you please. Tomorrow, after brunch, we'll meet and see what you came up with. You have until then to finish your assignment. Have fun today. The lake is beautiful."

"I hope I can come up with something by then," Kim confessed.

"Me, too," Denise muttered.

"You will," Julia said. "I have no doubts. You might want to work together if that'll help."

"If I can come up with a rite of passage, anyone can," Marge announced.

Kate was astonished. "You've already gotten something?"

"Do you find that hard to believe?" Marge grinned. "Of course, I have to refine it a little and throw in some details, but basically, I'm done."

"You probably have to refine it a lot," Kate mumbled.

"What was that?"

"Nothing. I'm just jealous because you have an idea and I don't."

Julia was leaving the room when she suddenly turned back. "Not to interrupt, but, before I forget, I've got a proposal. If you'd like to take advantage of Tahoe's night life, we made arrangements for dinner at Ceasar's followed by a k.d. Lang show."

Kim jumped to her feet. "Are you serious? Count me in. I'd never miss a chance to see her in concert."

"Isn't she that queer singer?" Marge sneered.

"Jesus, Marge. She's not queer."

"I forgot. I need to be more aware. Isn't she that lesbian singer?"

"Yes, she is," Denise answered, "and she's got the most terrific voice in the world. I'm in, too, but Marge, you probably won't like her. Why don't you stay here?"

"I'm going," Kate announced. "Ronald and I tried once to get tickets to see her, but she was sold out in twenty minutes."

They all looked at Marge.

"Okay, I'm going. I've heard her a couple of times. She's not bad—for a lesbian."

Kate laughed. "Gee, Marge. I think the lady does protest too much. Are you sure you aren't a closet lesbian?"

"Hell, no. I like men!"

"Just keep telling yourself that," Denise said.

"Ladies," Julia cut in, "I'm certain you can find better ways to enjoy the day. Tonight's festivities aren't formal, but if you brought something special to wear, tonight will be your only chance."

"Like a special pair of cowboy boots without manure on them?" Kim joked.

"When does the show start?" Marge asked.

"Whenever we're ready!" the others chimed.

Julia nodded and laughed as she left the room.

One by one, the women finished breakfast and left separately. Kim felt she should spend time in her office, but she couldn't imagine staying indoors on such a glorious day. She didn't have any ideas, anyway. Maybe being outside in the clean, crisp air would help her think clearly. She could do something with Bailey. He was always helpful.

She hurried back to camp, grabbed a leash, Bailey's treats and her camera. She found her backpack and started loading things she'd need for a long hike.

When she opened the refrigerator, she found oranges, apples, grapes and mineral water. As she closed the door, she shook her head. She didn't remember all that fruit being in there the previous night. Perhaps she forgot.

She knelt and squeezed Bailey. "It seems they know what we want before we want it."

He barked and wagged his tail.

When they left the campsite, Kim took pictures of the lake, making certain Bailey was in as many as possible.

"Wish I were an artist. I'd love to be able to paint something like this."

Kim and Bailey trudged through the woods. The sun was up and the water sparkled. It was blue in some places and green in others. The blend of colors was breathtaking. Bailey chased chipmunks and lizards every step of the way. At times, he seemed to chase make-believe critters, making Kim wonder if there were things she couldn't see. She enjoyed the hike, and Bailey loved dashing in and out of the water.

They stopped to rest around noon. The sun was high in the sky. It bothered Kim, not knowing what time it was. Without a watch, it seemed like there were more than twenty-four hours in a day. Maybe that was a good thing.

Kim climbed on a rock overlooking the lake. Down below her was a nice, quiet, secluded beach. She scrambled down the hill and stretched out on the sand. Bailey lay beside her and slept.

She talked to him as if he were listening.

"Did you notice if our car was outside the tent this morning? I don't remember seeing it. It doesn't matter. We don't need it and I wouldn't know how to get it out—there's no road."

She looked at him, but he didn't move. "Oh, you don't care. You're having a great time. If I'm not around, Karen is. I can't believe you're so comfortable with her. It's like you know her. Are you going to help me with this project? I don't know what I think about turning fifty. In some ways, I'm excited, because its a milestone. There are a lot of great women fifty and older."

Bailey moaned and rolled over. Kim munched on an apple.

"What would we like to do for my fiftieth? It's not that far away. You'd have to be there, and Linda. We need to do something outdoors. I wish my family could be there, too, sharing the excitement with me. That's probably asking too much."

She watched Bailey sleep. "I'll set my celebration up to be the ideal one for me. I'll invite everyone who's important in my life, including my folks. Then, if someone doesn't want to celebrate with me, I'd still be doing what I wanted. And, I'd know who my friends were."

Kim rose to her feet. "Come on, Bailey, let's keep walking. I might be onto something."

Along the way, Kim took pictures and marked the route in case they got lost.

"We're such creatures of habit, Bailey. We always mark our trail, even when we know where we're going, but we've never gotten lost, have we? Maybe it's in knowing that we marked the trail that makes it easier to find our way back."

She admitted to herself it was special to return to an old trail and find her marks still there. She never hurt trees or vegetation. It was reassuring to know she'd been there before.

*   *   *   *

Kate adjourned to her office after breakfast and spent several hours trying to reach anyone in New York. She wanted to touch base with someone familiar and get help with her rite of passage. Unfortunately, she was unable to reach anyone. She hadn't received any messages in return, either, so she sent more. Then she remembered Gwen.

"She has to be home. She had surgery the other day and said she'd be home for at least a week. She doesn't believe in answering machines, either."

Kate dialed and heard a friendly, "Hi."

"Hi, Gwen...."

"Tom and I can't come to the phone right now, but please leave a brief message, and we'll get back to you."

"Damn, Gwen! When did you sell out and get a stupid answering machine? You said you'd rot in hell first. Are you listening? Pick up the phone. Why aren't you home? This is Kate. I'm at Lake Tahoe. Give me a call when you get in. My number is...."

The machine shut off.

"Shit." Kate redialed, but the line was busy and remained so for the next hour.

"Either there's something wrong with Gwen's machine, or

Julia's messing with my calls. She said we wouldn't be able to tell anyone why we're here, but how does she know what I'm saying?"

She was nervous. "I feel trapped. Maybe Julia has everything bugged, or maybe there are hidden cameras. If I could just get started on my rite of passage, I'd feel better, but I don't have a clue. What would happen if I didn't come up with anything? I'd feel like an idiot in front of the others."

She threw up her hands and decided to return to her quarters. She could think as easily by the pool as in her office. Maybe relaxing would help.

Kate put on her bathing suit and picked up a notepad and pencil. At the last minute, she grabbed the Mick Jagger biography she'd been reading for the past three years. After taking a towel from the cupboard, she went to the pool and dove in.

The water was warmer than she expected. It felt good and she swam numerous laps. When she came out, she plopped into a lounge chair. She picked up the book and read the beginning lines.

"He is, without question, one of the dominant cultural figures of our time. Swaggering, strutting, sometimes sinister, always fascinating, Mick Jagger boasts a career spanning four decades, from the turbulent sixties and sybaritic seventies through the booming eighties and cautious nineties."

Kate liked Jagger's music, but she couldn't figure out what made him so special. He wasn't any more special than she was, except for the fact of telling everyone about it.

Maybe that's it," she mused. "I need to swagger and strut and tell the world I'm special."

She read further and found two years earlier, he turned fifty.

"He makes a big deal out of everything he does. Why can't I make a big deal out of this one important thing that'll happen to me? If I'm special, I should be able to show it."

She thought back over her life. Much of it was devoted to law.

"I have to come up with something. I have a brilliant legal mind. Maybe I'm trying to be too precise. That dingy Marge already has her rite of passage. How hard can it be?"

She leaned back in her chair and laid down the book. A moment later, she lurched upright. "I'll call Marge. I'd like to see the penthouse she's been raving about. Maybe I can get some ideas from her."

Kate ran inside, took the portable phone on the deck and dialed Marge's number.

"Hello?"

"Marge?"

"No, this is Maddie. Who's this?"

"Kate. Is Marge there?"

"No, she went out. Can I take a message?"

"No, thanks. I'll talk to her later."

Kate hung up and called Denise.

"Hello?"

"Denise?"

"Yeah. Who's this?"

"Kate."

"Hi. What are you doing?"

"Well, I spent several hours trying to contact someone in the outside world, but without success. I'm stuck in this project. I was so desperate, I called Marge, but she's not in. How are you doing?"

"Not very well."

"Why don't you grab your things and come over? Maybe we can help each other. I'm out back by the pool."

When Denise arrived, she wasn't wearing a swimsuit.

"Where's your suit?" Kate asked.

"To be honest, I don't own one."

Kate peered over her dark glasses, then handed her the phone. "Call your personal guide. She'll get you one."

"Ah, well, you see.... I don't have a suit, because I figured I'm too big to look good in one."

Kate removed her glasses. "Don't be ridiculous. Who cares if you look like Christie Brinkley? Let down your hair and enjoy yourself. You need to be more comfortable with who you are. If you aren't, those around you can't be, either."

"Sure, easy for you to say. You look like a fashion model."

"God. Am I that skinny? Then I shouldn't be in a suit, either. Go check in the bathhouse. I'll bet there's a suit for you. I hope it's brightly colored, too. That'll cheer you up."

A few minutes later, Denise emerged wrapped in a long bathrobe.

"What are you doing?" Kate asked.

Denise strutted to the side of the pool, then tore off the robe and shouted "Geronimo!" and did a cannonball into the pool, splashing water all over Kate.

Kate sat up sputtering, "Jesus, Denise. What got into you?"

Denise hoisted herself out of the pool. "I'm letting myself go. Look at this suit. Did you order it especially for me?"

Kate laughed. The suit's background was black, but it was streaked with huge stripes of fluorescent green and pink. As the two women grinned at each other, Kate surmised the suit was probably the ugliest thing she ever saw, but somehow, on Denise, it looked great.

"Wow! You look marvelous, Darling."

"Sure, like a giant beach ball." Denise sat in a lounge chair. "Your place is great, Kate. Can you believe how perfect the weather is?"

"Wonder if it's like this all the time?"

Denise giggled, "Or if Julia ordered it special for us."

"I wouldn't put it past her. How do you think she does it?"

"I have no idea. I can't figure it out, and somehow, I feel it's best if I don't know."

"You may be right."

"I haven't been able to reach anyone, either," Denise said. "You'd think someone would call us to make sure we arrived okay."

"That does seem strange, unless someone has called, and Julia told them we weren't available."

"All I've been able to do is leave phone messages, and they always get cut off."

"Does it happen just when you're going to explain why you're here?"

"I don't remember. Why?"

"It happens to me," Kate explained. "I was wondering if Julia is monitoring our calls. When we're about to say something she doesn't like, she cuts us off."

"I don't think so. I got cut off because I was too long-winded. Besides, Julia said we could talk about it after we leave."

"How far have you gotten with your rite of passage?"

"About as far as your pool."

"Me, too. I've had a lot more on my mind than turning fifty."

"You think that's bad, I lied to everyone I know about my age. No one knows I'll be fifty this year, except Gene."

"It wouldn't bother me so much that I don't have an idea, but Marge has one already. I can't believe she got one before me."

"Yeah, but can you imagine what her plan is?"

"Probably an all-night orgy with beer and men only."

"All of them under twenty-five."

"Even more reason to come up with something," Kate noted.

"She'll come up with something that works for her, and I'm certain there are women who'll identify with that, but we need something that will appeal to women like ourselves. Stop and think. What would you do to announce it to the world that you're fifty and making a big deal out of it?"

Denise was lost in thought. "I don't know. Maybe I'd have a special awards presentation, not as extravagant as the Academy Awards, but with the same kind of fuss. They could give me a statue or a plaque."

"Who's they?"

"How do I know? Doesn't Julia have someone to do that? Perhaps not. Maybe I could start an organization which would sponsor such things. I could get women from around the country to join. They might even donate money for the awards."

"If the women couldn't come to the presentation, someone could at least buy the award and make a presentation," Kate said. "You know, that sounds like the start of a great idea."

Okay, now what about you? What would you do to celebrate?"

"My idea is to write to your organization and have them send a plaque and the bill to my company," Kate laughed.

"There must be something in legalese you could do."

"Legalese?"

"I don't know what else to call it."

Kate pondered. "You could publish a legal notice in the paper, announcing your arrival into the second half of womanhood. It could be a combination engagement and birth announcement. It would be the social event of the year. We publish notices for other things like death, marriages, and graduations. Then, I'd have an open house for everyone to stop by and congratulate the relic."

Denise smiled. "There's no need to be cynical. You have the start of something."

"Maybe you're right. I better start writing some of this down before I forget it."

Me, too. Can I borrow some paper?"

*   *   *   *

Marge finished breakfast and went back to her penthouse and to bed. She didn't know how long she slept, but she felt better. She decided to explore the grounds and see where the others were staying.

As she reached the trail, she said, "I wish I had a horse to ride."

She turned and found a horse tied to a tree. She mounted him and stared at the saddle. It was an exact copy of her own saddle, including the nick in the saddle horn and the slash on the cinch belt she put there by accident. She shook her head and rode down the trail.

She was most curious about Kim's tent, so she asked for directions there. Trees surrounded her, and she searched for an opening, hoping to see the castle from afar.

"I'll know my penthouse when I see it," she said. "I left a blue towel on the balcony rail."

When she emerged into Kim's clearing, she was shocked. "Wow. What a layout. I never realized camping could be so regal."

After finding Kim gone, she investigated the tent and the bathhouse. "She's got everything she could want, except a casino. It's cute."

Marge remounted her horse and headed for Kate's. Again, she was surprised. "Looks like no matter what we chose, we all got star treatment."

She heard Kate and Denise chatting by the pool but decided not to stop. Instead, she rode to Denise's bungalow. This time, she wasn't surprised.

"I knew hers would be as luxurious as the rest. There's no doubt that when Julia sets things up, she does it in style."

Marge loved the bungalow and almost wished she had chosen it. Still, she had the penthouse, and no one else did.

She kept riding, but no matter where she went, she never caught a glimpse of the castle. In fact, she didn't see any buildings.

"This must be some kind of trick, but there has to be a logical explanation. Julia's the only one who knows."

After her ride, Marge decided to go shopping. She won several hundred dollars the previous night and wanted to buy gifts.

"Who knows? Maybe I'll win some more tonight. I wouldn't mind running into Frank again. After I shop, I'll go see if he's around. There's still plenty of time for some afternoon delight."

CHAPTER TWENTY-ONE

It was growing dark when the women met in the castle lobby. Julia and Hildy were waiting.

"Perfect timing, Ladies," Julia said. "We just arrived. Hope you had a marvelous day. The limousine awaits."

They climbed inside and headed toward town and the hotel/casino.

Marge looked out the darkened windows in the back seat.

"Maybe someone will think we're celebrities."

"Only if they can't see who we really are," Denise said.

"There are a lot of limousines in Lake Tahoe," Julia pointed out. "However, if anyone asks, feel free to sign autographs."

"Right. Whose names do we sign?" Denise asked.

"I've been told I look a lot like Loretta Swit," Marge said.

"Yes, I see the resemblance," Kate commented. "Hot lips."

When they arrived at the casino, they were ushered into the lobby and escorted to the main headliner room. Their table was on the first level up, directly in front of the stage.

Kim looked around. "These must be the best seats in the house."

"I hope so," Julia smiled.

They were treated like celebrities during dinner. The four women were getting along so well that Julia was often left out. It didn't bother her. One of her goals was to bring the women closer.

The show began after dinner. k.d. Lang entertained for almost two hours. The women were thrilled with the show. Marge gave the entertainer a standing ovation after each number, and her ear-splitting whistles echoed throughout the room.

On their way to the lobby after the show, Kim walked next to Julia. "Thank you for dinner and that marvelous show. I loved it."

Kate and Denise expressed their gratitude, too.

"I have to admit," Marge stated, "I've never heard a voice like hers. She's better than Patsy Cline, and I thought she had the best voice in the world. Thank you, Julia."

"Ladies, it was my pleasure."

Marge turned to Kim. "I'm sorry about all those cracks about queers. You probably know they were made out of ignorance. I'm sorry."

"My, how you've mellowed in two days," Kate observed.

Marge put her arm around Kim as they kept walking. "Hell, I haven't mellowed. I like Kim. The things I said before were stupid. I've learned a lot from you all. I hope I leave here with a better understanding about a lot of things."

"Thank you, Marge. I accept your apology."

"Well, you could've said a lot about my lifestyle, but you didn't."

"Don't worry. I'd never call you a slut."

"I know, but I deserved it."

"Come on, Marge," Denise said. "Don't be so hard on yourself."

Marge told them about her trek to the casino to find Frank for a little afternoon rendezvous.

"Be sure to change the sheets after she leaves," Kate advised.

"Is screwing all you think about?" Kim asked.

"I'm not proud of what I did," Marge confessed, "but I'm going through a tough time. I'm not dead yet. My body's changing and I don't understand the changes. My personal life is a shambles. I don't know what to do. I'm starting to feel old, and I don't like it."

When they reached the limousine, everyone took the same seats.

"No one likes getting old," Denise said. "I'm more afraid of growing old than of dying. At least when you die, it's over. You won't suffer anymore. The thought of becoming a vegetable and not being able to do things for myself is frightening."

"I'd rather lose my mind than my body," Kate added.

"Me, too," Kim said.

"Why?" Marge asked.

"If I lose my mind, I won't know it. I wouldn't know I was old, or that anything was wrong with me."

Kim nodded, "I'd rather die than sit in a wheelchair all day and know I couldn't hike or camp. It would be horrible to have an alert mind with a body that couldn't do anything."

"Julia," Marge said, "maybe you can help us. You're much older. How'd you grow old so gracefully?"

The other women cringed.

"She'll always have rough edges," Kate said.

Julia turned in the front seat. "Who says I did it gracefully? The mind and the body are important. I did as many things as I could, medically and otherwise, to try and preserve my youth. Truth is, I can't do all the things I could when I was twenty, and I can only do a few of the things I could do at fifty."

"That must be hard," Denise said.

Julia laughed. "It's not all bad. While I can't ski anymore, I also don't make the same stupid mistakes I made at twenty. I may not get any afternoon delight like Marge, but I know and understand so much more than I did at fifty. I'm more at peace with myself, too."

"You're one hundred," Denise pointed out. "What keeps you going?"

"Your perspective changes as you age. I no longer enjoy watching people do things I used to do. I'm not a good spectator anymore. Living has a new, more significant meaning. That's not to say I don't miss being young, but one finds other things."

"Like what?" Kim asked.

"I took art lessons and learned how to paint. I was going to write a book until the idea for a rite of passage came to me. It took a long time to organize this. I often feared I wouldn't live to see it through."

"Are you sorry you did it?" Marge asked.

Julia smiled, "Not for a second. The more I watch you women, the more I know this was one of the best ideas I ever had. Thank you. It has been a treat for me. I'll miss you when this is over."

"Oh, no," Denise cried. "We should thank you. I can't speak for the others, but I've been helped more than you know. We'll miss you, too, but we'll stay in touch."

"How'd you get the money to finance this?" Kate wanted to know.

"Money is no object. I do hope the four of you will keep in close touch."

They arrived at the castle late, but no one felt tired. They left the limousine and waved goodnight.

"Remember that brunch will be early tomorrow," Julia warned. "We have business to finish."

Marge roared with laughter. "Don't worry about me. I'm staying in tonight."

"What?" Kate said. "You've gone through all the men in Lake Tahoe?"

"No," Kim added, "she just did everything there was to do."

"Joke all you want," Marge grinned. "I can take it. Let's just say I'm trying to find new meaning to my life. Besides, I've got two men at home and I don't know what to do with them."

Julia disappeared into the castle. As the other women walked toward the trails leading to their quarters, Marge shouted, "Hey, guys!"

"Guys?" Kim questioned.

"Oops. Sorry about that. It's a North Dakota saying. I'm trying to clean up my act. It might take me a little longer because I've got further to go. Anyway, it's not that late. Why don't you come up to the penthouse? We could have a nightcap or snack. I have a surprise for you."

"I'll bet," Denise snickered. "What's his name?"

"No, really. Please come. I saw all your places today, and I'd like to show you mine."

"She's got a point," Kate said. "I'd love to see the penthouse."

"Yeah, let's go," Denise agreed.

"I love it," Kim chuckled. "From tent to penthouse. Sounds like the name of a book."

"Good. You can help me figure out how they put a fifteen-story penthouse in a three-story building. The view's tremendous at night."

They walked arm-in-arm to the lobby and the elevator. As the door closed behind them, Marge pushed the P button, and they headed for her suite.

CHAPTER TWENTY-TWO

"My God, Marge," Kim gasped. "This is beautiful."

"Pretty classy," Denise said eyeing the furniture.

"No kidding," Marge replied. "I've never seen anything like it. I feel so pampered. Come to the balcony. One of you has to help me."

They walked onto the balcony and enjoyed the view of the lake.

"What's the problem?" Denise asked. "You don't like the view?"

"I love it, but you've seen the outside of the castle. It's not possible to get a view like this from a building no more than three stories. According to my calculations, you need at least fifteen stories."

"You've got a point," Kim said. "You can't get this view from the castle. I haven't seen anything in the area that might be close to fifteen stories high."

"I rode around all morning," Marge added. "I didn't see any buildings from the woods, not even this one."

"Come to think of it," Kate continued, "I never see the castle once I hit the trail to my place."

"It's almost as if it doesn't exist," Denise said.

"We know it exists. We're in it," Marge pointed out."

"Maybe we could ask our guides about it," Denise suggested.

"Sure, but they are pretty useless when it comes to specifics," Kate said. "They know how to act dumb when they don't want to answer. And, they don't want to answer when it comes to wanting hard facts about this place."

"Forget the guides," Marge instructed. "Forget that everyone here knows what we want before we do. I'm talking about a visible, tangible thing. I want to know where this penthouse is. It exists, but it can't be part of the castle. So, where are we?"

They were silent, gazing into the night and watching lights flicker on the lake.

"Watch this," Marge announced. "If you think the penthouse thing is strange, follow me."

She led them to the double doors they entered minutes earlier.

"Have you seen any hint of a casino around here?" Marge queried. "There should be people, noise, a parking lot full of cars.... It hit me when we were in Ceasar's tonight. It was noisy, had lots of people. Watch."

She put her hand on the doorknob. "I'd like to take my friends to the casino." She opened the door and led them inside.

Kate became upset. "We get the idea, Marge. Let's get out of here."

"What's the matter?" Kim asked.

"I don't know, but this isn't right. Everything is strange and getting worse."

"Has it ever occurred to any of you that none of this is real?" Denise asked.

"Sure," Marge answered, "like we're having a simultaneous dream?"

"Denise might be onto something," Kate said. "It's not a dream, but maybe an extension of time that brought us together."

"Yeah, like we're watching the same movie, but we're all in

164

it, too," Denise stated.

"That's stupid," Marge said. "It would be like saying none of this happened. We never flew to Tahoe, and Julia doesn't exist."

"I don't know what to think," Kim said. "There are a lot of strange things happening. What about our guides? None of them has a real job. This is the first time my guide has worked for Julia, yet she feels close to her. She's too much like me, even implied we've been together before. I'll bet they're here now, but we can't see them. They're always present."

"Mine wants me to believe she's my guardian angel," Denise offered.

"Mine implied she'd been with me all my life," Marge added.

"Mine too," Kim confirmed. "So, what do we do? What purpose do they have for us?"

Kate was thoughtful. "I don't think we have anything to worry about. There has been nothing of a threatening nature happen so far. We've all been through some rough times lately. Maybe this is a way of...what should I call it? Divine providence is guiding us, helping us get our lives together."

"Could be," Denise agreed. "Why us? Maybe this same thing is happening to other women somewhere else."

"By getting a few of us together to solve our problems and create a rite of passage, we'll somehow help other women get their shit together? Do you realize how corny that sounds?" Kim asked.

"Maybe this is what happens when women go through menopause," Marge suggested. "We're taken somewhere to evaluate our lives and our future. That would explain why they say women go crazy during menopause. It probably happens to everyone."

"We have to pump our guides for more information," Kate said. "We need their full names and what they know about Julia and the castle. They're the key to all this."

"I talked to mine," Kim offered. "If she knows anything, she's not talking. She's more concerned about what I'm going through with my family and all."

Denise raised her hand as if she had an idea. "Maybe that's part of why you're here, to come up with a plan to mend the rift between you and your family."

"If you can do that," Kate said, "it might help others in similar situations. I imagine to your family, being gay is one of the worst things you can be."

"There are times when I think Mom would be happier if I were a whore," Kim stated. "But, I'm not the only one with a problem. If we could, as Kate says, get our lives together, we would've accomplished something, even if it didn't help anyone else. I feel like my life's been going nowhere. This weekend has given me the courage to try and fix some things."

Marge started to laugh. "I have this image of Julia sitting somewhere, nodding and smiling, saying 'I did well.'"

The others laughed with her.

"I feel like someone's pushing and guiding me without my being aware of it," Marge explained.

"There's a definite reason the four of us are together in this," Kate said.

Marge waved her hand, "We should exchange addresses and phone numbers so we can keep in touch when this is over. I'll ask Julia if we can call or write her sometime. After all, we don't know how much longer she'll be around to keep tabs on us."

"Good point," Denise said. "We don't know much about her, but I assume she plans to keep track of us when we leave."

"Do you think she bugged our places?" Kate wondered.

"Probably," Marge looked around. "She must have hidden cameras, too, because she always knows what we're doing. I was so sure, I started winking in the mirror to her and waving at make-believe cameras to let her know I know she's here. I no longer worry about it. She's taking care of us."

Marge walked to the nearest mirror and waved. "See, Julia? We're trying to live up to your expectations."

The others laughed and glanced nervously at the mirror.

"Tomorrow we present our ideas to her," Kim said. "Is everyone ready?"

They nodded.

"Great," she moaned. "I'm not sure what I'm going to do. At least after tonight, I have a few more ideas. Hopefully, I'll be able to articulate them by tomorrow."

"If you need help, let us know," Kate offered.

"Are we supposed to write these down or talk about them?" Denise questioned.

"Julia never said. I don't think it matters," Kate replied, "as long as we have something."

Marge brought out business cards and passed them around. In return, she collected everyone else's address and phone number.

"Has anyone thought about the possibility that if this place doesn't exist, we might not be able to leave?" Denise asked.

"Not even once," Kim responded quickly.

"Julia wouldn't do that to us," Kate added.

"Please," Marge begged. "You're being overly imaginative. "We're leaving tomorrow, and I have a little something for each of you."

"You're kidding," Denise replied.

"Marge, we didn't expect...." Kate began.

"Now, don't get mushy or cynical on me. I won a little at the casino last night, so I spent it today. I found a great gift shop, and, well, I found something for all of us to remind us of this weekend."

"When did you go to town?" Kim asked.

"Didn't have to. I said I wanted to visit a gift shop, opened the door, and there I was. Here."

Denise opened hers immediately. It was a gold chain with a small pendant hanging from it. "Marge, it's darling. It's a tiny castle."

The others opened theirs and found the same miniature castles on chains.

"It's real gold, too," Marge beamed.

"Thank you." Kim hugged her.

"You shouldn't have," Kate said.

Marge shrugged them off. "I told you I won money, and they weren't that expensive. It was kind of strange—the store, I mean. I didn't know what to expect, and it was like these castles drew me like a magnet. There were only four of them."

Kim stood with her arm around Marge. "This is sweet of you, no matter whose money it was. I'll cherish this. I have a present for all of you, too, but it's not ready yet. "I've taken rolls and rolls of pictures. When I get them developed, I'll send copies to everyone."

Denise stood. "I'll have plaques made to celebrate our coming into womanhood. I'll send you one when they're done."

Kate was subdued. "What can I get for you to show my appreciation?"

"You're a legal whiz," Marge noted. "Why don't you put some of your experts and resources together and see what you can find out about Julia and this castle? Then, when you solve the mystery, you can share it with us?"

Kate hesitated. "I guess I could. It shouldn't be too difficult to track down. She must have had a husband, maybe even some children. If you're willing to accept my solving the mystery as my gift to you, I'd love the challenge."

The women helped Marge clean up after their snacks. A bond had been formed, and all of them felt satisfied and fulfilled. The support they felt from each other was something none of them expected after their first introduction.

Each woman put on her gold chain and marveled at how good the pendants looked. They were convinced Julia had set Marge up to win the money and buy the gifts. They stood at the door of the penthouse in a group hug. Marge waved to the mirror in case Julia was watching.

"A show of unity for her highness," Marge bowed.

They expressed sadness that the next day would be the end of their conference, but they discussed plans to get together at a later date, in Lake Tahoe, and perhaps, in each other's home towns.

"It's too bad Julia couldn't have placed us closer together, instead of all over the country," Denise lamented.

"Maybe she'd lend us that jet and the pilot for the next get-together," Marge said.

"I'm sure," Denise said.

"Maybe she doesn't want us to get together after this," Kate suggested.

"No," Kim said. "She said she hoped we'd keep in touch with each other. I think Julia intended big things for us. After all, we share the same birth date."

"And time," Marge added.

CHAPTER TWENTY-THREE

Kim was up early. Even though she'd been up late the night before, she felt rested. Bailey crawled onto the bed in the middle of the night and snuggled next to her with his head on the pillow. He groaned when she rolled over.

Kim looked out the window and saw the first hint of light flickering through the trees.

"Come, Bailey. Let's walk before breakfast. The others won't be up for hours."

Bailey yawned. He stretched, but didn't move off the bed. Kim slipped into Levi's and hiking boots, then pulled on a sweater.

"Get up, Bailey. It's a beautiful morning.

He didn't move.

"You might find some chipmunks."

His eyes rolled forward. He knew about chipmunks. They chattered at him to get his attention, then, when he charged, they dove into their burrows and laughed at him.

He was at the door before Kim had her jacket on. When she opened the flap, he lunged out, his head swiveling as he searched for critters.

The morning air was crisp and fresh. The smell of pine lingered in the air, and Kim took a deep breath as they headed down the path.

"This weekend has been strange."

Bailey scampered ahead, ignoring her.

"I wouldn't have missed it for anything. It's been like a fantastic dream. No, more than that. For all its weirdness, there has been an undercurrent of serenity and understanding I haven't felt in a long time. The only thing better would've been if Linda could've shared it with us."

*　　*　　*　　*

Marge rolled over in bed, opened one eye to glance at the clock, then realized it was futile to try and tell the time. She was getting accustomed to operating without a time frame. She knew it was early—the sun was barely up—but she felt rested and ready for the day. She reached over and opened the drapes. The lake was still there, fifteen stories down.

She didn't want to sleep anymore, so she crawled out of bed. She opened the sliding door and walked onto the patio to stretch.

"I need some coffee."

She went into the kitchen and found the coffee maker all set up, ready to go.

"Must have been Maddie." She pushed the button. She watched, transfixed, as hot, dark liquid dripped into the pot. When she reached for a cup, she found one that read, *Rites of Passage Castle.*

"That's neat." She held it gently in her hands. "I wonder if Julia would miss it?" She looked around for a camera. "Oh, hell. She'd know if anything were missing. She knows everything."

When the coffee was ready, she poured a cup and walked back to the patio.

"I know the others aren't far from here, but I can't see their places. Why can't they see the castle? It's like we're in our own worlds, somewhere apart from each other."

She touched the necklace and smiled. "They were surprised when I gave them their castles. I'm glad I did it. Every time we look at these things, it'll remind us of our time together."

*   *   *   *

Denise didn't want to get up. She was comfortable in a warm, toasty bed. She wasn't anxious to start Sunday, because it was the last day at the castle and she didn't want to go home. It had been the most unusual weekend of her life.

However, she didn't want to miss out on anything, either. She wanted to see her new friends again. She was amazed at how close she felt toward them in such a short time. She didn't make friends easily, but these women were different.

"I even feel close to Marge." She fingered the necklace. She laughed and thought of the four of them.

"I never would have chosen any of them to be my friend if we met in Dallas."

She wrote in her diary. Suddenly, she realized her diary took a new direction. It was as if she were writing to Gene. She liked the fact that her feelings for him had grown to a new level. She set down her pen and got up. She made the bed even though she was certain a maid would come in and do it for her. She didn't want anyone to think of her as sloppy.

Denise hummed as hot water from the shower splashed over her. As she dressed, she began to hurry. She knew the others were up, heading toward brunch. She didn't want to miss them.

Before she walked down the trail, she turned to look at the bungalow. She was sad that she had spent her last night there.

"I hope Kim got a picture of it for me. If I could ever have a vacation home, I'd want it exactly like this. Gene would love it, too."

*   *   *   *

Even before Kate opened her eyes, she reached for the remote control and turned on the TV. She hadn't heard any news for days. Somehow, she wasn't surprised when she couldn't find any of the regular shows like Meet the Press, or Sunday Morning.

"Julia must have her own broadcasting network. She doesn't put on anything that'll give us a clue about the rest of the world. I don't even know if today's Sunday."

She got out of bed and went into the kitchen for a glass of orange juice. She remembered her vitamins and retrieved them from the bathroom. She touched the gold castle around her neck.

"Whoever would've thought Marge would do something like that?"

She walked onto the deck. It was a beautiful morning, full of sunshine. Ronald would love a place like this. Maybe she could bring him here. Perhaps Julia rented the place when she wasn't giving conferences.

Finally, Kate dressed and walked toward the castle. She didn't want to be the last to arrive.

The women entered the lobby at the same time.

Kate laughed, "We have to stop meeting like this."

"What will people think," Marge agreed. "No matter what we do, we always end up at the same place at the same time."

The dining room doors opened, and Julia emerged. "Good morning, Ladies. We have a lovely brunch set up for you. Help yourself. If you want something you don't see...."

"Ask for it!" the women chorused.

Julia was jubilant. "By Jove, I think you've got it."

They found one of the most lavish brunches they'd ever seen. There were four large tables, filled with every breakfast, lunch or snack item imaginable.

"I've seen some fancy brunches in my day," Kate observed, "but I have never seen anything like this."

Denise stared at the food. "I dare anyone to think of something that's not on one of these tables."

They filled their plates and sat at the round table with Julia.

"May I ask something?" Denise queried.

"Of course," Julia replied.

"What will you do with all that food? I appreciate all the choices, but we can't eat even part of what's there."

"I'm glad you're concerned, but don't worry, it won't go to waste. We donate all our leftovers to a local homeless shelter. There are many who will enjoy what you can't eat."

"Is there a large homeless group here?" Kate asked.

"Yes. More than you'd think. Our weather is cold much of the year. I often wonder how they survive."

Kate watched Julia carefully.

"Is there something on your mind, Kate?" Julia asked.

"Kind of. Do...do you have any children?"

"All of you are my children."

"I meant children of your own."

Julia became sullen, "I never did."

"Were you married?" Marge blurted.

"Now, Ladies. We aren't here to discuss me," Julia waved. "This is your weekend, and we still have unfinished business. By the way, Marge, those necklaces you bought are charming. I'm sure you'll cherish them forever."

"I'm glad you like them." Marge leaned closer to show hers to Julia. "You enjoy letting me know you know what I'm up to, don't you?"

Julia smiled. "I'm not trying to rush you. Please take your time and enjoy yourselves, but I must excuse myself to do a few things. When you're through, finish your rites of passage. I hope you'll put them in writing so you can take them with you when you leave. We'll meet in the garden conference room for lunch and to share your ideas."

Julia excused herself and left.

"I have an idea," Kate said. "Let's work together on our final proposals."

"Good idea," Denise agreed. "Where?"

"How about my office? I have everything we could need," Kate offered. "We can print out our final rites on the computer."

Kim nodded. "The least we can do is make a big presentation out of this. It is why we were invited."

Let's ask our guides to find some nice file folders to put them in," Denise suggested.

"We'll make copies for ourselves and one for Julia," Marge added.

They finished eating and started for the door, but Marge and Kim ran back to grab extra muffins and fresh fruit.

CHAPTER TWENTY-FOUR

"Okay, Marge," Kate directed. "You were the first to come up with an idea, so let's start with you."

"Mine is simple," Marge started. "I want to throw a big party and invite everyone in town. I'll rent the Veteran's Memorial Hall, hire a band, cater food, sell drinks to defray costs, and hope everyone brings me a present."

"That's simple?" Denise giggled. "What do you get out of it?"

"Recognition from lots of people, and a wild party. You might not be the partying type, but I am. This is a great excuse for a bash. I never had a real party, not even as a kid. No one ever made a fuss over me. I'd like for that to happen."

The women started writing and rewriting until they had a formal proposal for Marge's rite of passage. Marge silently read it once the computer printed it out.

"This sounds good," she declared. "In fact, you made it sound better than I could have."

"Anything you want changed?" Kate asked.

"No. This is exactly what I want."

The women congratulated each other.

"Who's next?" Kate queried.

"Let's do yours," Denise suggested.

"Sure. I'm ready. I want to run a public legal notice in the paper—actually, the New York Times—and announce my arrival into womanhood."

She showed her proposal to the group, and Kim wrinkled her nose.

"This sounds awfully formal...almost like an obituary. Why don't you lighten it up and have some fun? This should be a joyous occasion."

"Yeah," Marge contributed. "Run a picture of yourself."

"I know," Denise shouted. "Do it like when people announce an engagement or wedding."

"Not bad," Kate laughed. "I can just see it. People will see the picture and wonder what this old lady is doing announcing her engagement. Then they'll read it and wonder how any woman dared show her face for a menopause announcement"

"It'll take guts, but you'd be the first," Marge stated.

"I like it. I never had my picture in the paper when I got married. You're right, Kim. This is the time to let my hair down."

"So what if anyone thinks it's strange," Denise said. "We always get explained away as being strange, anyway, because we're going through the change of life."

"Is that all?" Marge asked. "Just an announcement in the paper?"

"No, there's more. I'm going to have a reception at my house for invited guests and family, like they do after a wedding."

"Will they bring presents?" Marge continued.

"Why not? I wouldn't mind."

"You could go to a store and register a pattern, just like a bride," Denise teased.

"Right."

"Hey, I thought of that first, but Maddie told me it was tacky," Marge quipped.

178

The women concentrated on the wording of Kate's proposal. When it came off the printer, she was pleased. "I like it," Kate smiled.

"I'll go next," Kim offered. "I have an idea, but I need some help wording it."

"Great. What's the idea?" Kate asked.

"I want to plan something outdoors. I want to rent a houseboat at Lake Shasta. Then I'd invite my closest friends. We could spend the whole weekend fishing, swimming, hiking—you know, enjoying Mother Nature. We'd have time to reflect on things and make plans for the future. In the worst case, if no one came, I'd still be doing the things I love."

"That sounds like you," Denise said. "What about inviting your family?"

"I don't think they'd come."

"Why not?"

"Since Mom and I aren't on speaking terms, I have no idea how to get them there, and I don't think she'd want to spend the weekend with gay people."

"Are all your guests going to be gay?" Marge asked.

"No. I have some straight friends, too."

"Well, then," Denise added, "don't tell them who's gay and who's not. You can't tell by looking."

"That's not the problem," Kim sighed. "Mom wouldn't be able to deal with Linda and me."

"How do you know?" Kate asked. "Maybe if you had all those people together in a nonthreatening environment, loaded with fun and fellowship, your parents might have a good time."

"Your parents might be looking for the right opportunity to make peace with you," Marge stated. "With lots of people around, it might be easier than one-on-one."

"You might be right."

"Sounds like all you need to do is figure out the right way to invite them," Kate said.

"That's the hard part," Kim admitted, "but it's sure worth a try."

"Let's see if we can write this down and make it feasible," Kate suggested. "The details on the invitations can be worked out later."

When they finished the proposal, Kim was excited. "This is going to work. I'll call Karen and see if she can find something special to put this in."

Karen stuck her head in the doorway. "You wanted something?"

"What took you so long?"

Everyone laughed.

"We need a folder or binder to put our proposals in," Kim instructed.

"Like what?"

She shrugged, "I don't know, maybe something in a nice leather binder that looks luxurious. I don't want one that requires punching holes. I want a self-binding folder."

The others nodded in agreement.

"How many?" Karen asked.

"Five."

"Five?" Denise questioned.

"One for each of us and one for Julia. She'll love it."

Karen shut the door. Kate turned to Denise. "Okay, you're the only one left."

Denise stood. "Here goes. I want to have a special awards presentation of some kind."

"Like the Academy Awards?" Marge snickered.

Denise lifted her chin and looked into the distance. "Exactly." She walked around the room and gestured with her arms. "Maybe not exactly like the Academy Awards, but on that order. I want to be presented with a plaque celebrating my accomplishment. It should be something I can hang on the wall with my diploma and other awards."

"You have other awards?" Kim joked.

"Yes. They might not seem like much to you, but I've been recognized for my community work and by the accounting organization to which I belong."

"For what, making the fewest addition errors or having the fewest IRS audits?" Marge teased.

"Come on, Ladies," Kate interrupted. "Denise is serious. We need to help her formulate it."

"It should be easy to have a plaque made," Kim said. "Who'll present it?"

"I've given that a lot of thought," Denise replied. "I'm going to organize a group, like the Rites of Passage Foundation. It would be the foundation's job to sponsor this kind of thing and see that the presentations are made. They might be able to do it in conjunction with a women's gathering."

"Like what?" Kate asked.

"I don't know," Denise was irritated. "Maybe a National Organization of Women meeting, the American Association of University Women, Daughters of the American Revolution, Woman of the Year. Hell, I just came up with the idea. How am I supposed to know all the details?"

"That might be a good way to start with the presentations," Marge offered. "However, I see this growing so big, the foundation might have to plan its own events to make the presentations."

"Thanks, Marge, I like that."

"You might be able to carry it farther," Kate pointed out. "You don't have to stay in Dallas."

"What do you mean?"

"I want one of those plaques on my wall, and I have friends I'd like to give one to. Women all over the country are going to want one. You could set up chapters in major cities to help distribute the plaques. You could sell them to defray the foundation's expenses. People could order them as gifts for the women in their lives."

Kim was thoughtful. "You could make it a nonprofit foundation. Then you could accept donations from people and businesses. I bet a lot of companies would donate. Look how many cater to women now."

"Don't count on Kotex for any large donations," Marge said.

"Why not?" Kate demanded.

"Menopausal women don't use them anymore."

"That doesn't mean they wouldn't want to contribute. Look how much money they made off us over the years. It would make them look good to younger women, too."

"Then there are the companies making things like Depends," Denise added. "They think we'll lose control of our bladders as we age."

Kate sighed, "Just do your Kegle exercises six times a day and you won't have to worry."

"What?" Marge asked.

"Ask your doctor."

"You might even be able to get government funding," Kim continued. "They dole out millions for less worthy causes. And, who in their right mind would turn down a bunch of menopausal women?"

"I love it!" Denise shouted. "This is even better than I hoped for."

The women worked feverishly to organize their ideas and get them printed. As the final product came out, Kim noticed that Karen had quietly come in and placed some folders on the table. She went to pick them up.

"My God!" she exclaimed. "Look at these."

They were made of soft, brown leather, and the fronts and backs were padded. Inside was a strip where one could place papers. When the folder closed, the papers were bound inside.

On the cover, in gold-embossed, slightly raised, beautifully scripted letters, were the words, *Rite of Passage*.

"I knew she'd help us," Marge said. "Julia thinks of everything."

CHAPTER TWENTY-FIVE

No matter how much they convinced themselves that nothing at the castle could surprise them, they were still amazed when they walked into Julia's garden conference room. She waited for them at the gazebo.

"It's wonderful to see you again. I feel like I've known you forever," Julia was teary-eyed. "And, it seems you've become fast friends. I hope those bonds remain with you forever."

"Can you believe it?" Kate asked. "I wouldn't have given two cents for this group becoming close last Friday."

"It pleases me immensely. Sit down and order whatever you'd like for lunch."

Kate was unofficially designated as the spokeswoman for the group. She carried the leather folders. They were nervous as they faced Julia at the small table.

"I hope you've had a marvelous time," Julia said.

"It's been fantastic," Kim replied.

The others nodded.

"I've had great time," Marge confessed, "but, I can't go home with something still driving me crazy."

"What's that, Dear?" Julia smiled.

"How the hell did you get a penthouse suite fifteen stories off the ground in a building that's only three stories tall?"

Julia raised her head slowly, "Ah, my practical contractor. You haven't figured it out?"

"Apparently not. Don't tell me it's all in my head."

Julia looked at her blankly. "What would you like me to tell you? You're being too realistic. You asked for a penthouse, and that's what you got. You're the one who set the standard of a penthouse needing to be fifteen stories up, not me."

"You mean I'm really only on the third floor? How do you explain the view?"

"I haven't seen it. I can only assume it's something you'd expect at fifteen stories."

"The others have seen it," Marge persisted. She looked at them. "You all saw the view, didn't you?"

No one answered.

"There are many things in life which can't be explained, Marge," Julia continued. "Perhaps, as long as the experience was enjoyable, you should accept your own interpretation of it. Maybe the issue is more one of acceptance rather than questioning why you see things the way you do. I believe the others accept you without questioning why you are the way you are. That's probably why they saw what you did."

Marge had no response. Once their orders were lunch were delivered, Kate turned to Julia.

"You know everything about us, and we know so little about you."

"I'm not the one who's important," Julia answered. "You are. I'm merely the instrument by which you will go through your rite of passage."

"Yes, but where do you live. Are you here all year? Do you run seminars for a living? How did you find the money to sponsor this? Will you do more of them? Are any members of your family alive? What else have you done these past one hundred years?"

"Whoa! I understand your desire to know more about me, but I don't want you to lose your focus. I have many missions in life. Right now, my main one is trying to help women find themselves. You've been chosen as my messengers."

"Will we ever see you again?" Kim asked.

Julia was somber. "As much as I'd like that, I doubt it. I'm one hundred years old, and you have a lot to do when you leave here."

"Can't we keep in touch?" Denise pushed. "Can't we write or call?"

"Don't worry. I'll always be near. I'll stay in touch in my own way."

"I don't wish to be crass," Marge said, "but how will we know if something happens to you?"

"You'll know."

"Yes, but...." Kate began.

"Ladies, please finish your lunches."

The women ate silently. Each felt she was going to lose Julia and didn't know how to stop it. Julia ate little.

When everyone was finished, Kate asked, "Are you finished, Julia?"

"Yes."

"Here, take a look at these. We printed our rite of passage proposals on a computer and bound them in these. You might as well start reading."

"How wonderful." There were tears in Julia's eyes. "I've been interested in what you'd come up with. These are beautifully packaged. Nice touch."

"As if she didn't know," Marge muttered.

Julia read while the women finished their desserts. Her expression never changed. Each woman waited patiently, like a child in school waiting for her teacher's comments.

When Julia finished, she gently closed the folder, laid it on her lap, and raised her eyes toward the sky. Everyone looked up, but saw nothing.

As Julia lowered her eyes, a tear ran down her cheek. She stood slowly. "These are perfect. It's more than I hoped for."

The women grinned, looked at each other, and sighed. They felt relieved.

"I knew you wouldn't let me down," Julia continued. "I'm thrilled with the seriousness with which you approached the assignment. While I expected some answer from you, I never expected anything this complete and so well thought out. Ladies, you made my mission a success. My only hope is that you'll follow through with your ideas and continue to grow as women and human beings."

"Thank you," Kate said. "We hoped you'd be pleased, but we approached the task as something we'd do for ourselves."

"I can tell. Thank you."

"One copy is for you," Denise added.

"Thank you. I'll cherish this more than you'll ever know." She stood and walked away.

"Where are you going?" Kim called.

Julia turned and waved. She was crying. "You've made me happy, but my job here is done. The rest is up to you. I must go." She threw them a kiss and walked out of sight.

"Are we going to let her leave like that?" Denise was adamant.

"I don't think we have a choice," Kim said thoughtfully.

"What did she mean?" Kate asked.

"It sounded like she was going off to die," Marge stated.

Denise stood. "Oh, God, I hope not. Maybe we should go after her. I don't want things to end like this."

A hand touched her shoulder. It was Danielle. "Julia's fine. Don't go after her."

"Where'd she go?" Denise demanded.

"It's not important. Trust me. What is important is for all of you to get on with your lives. The last few hours here are yours to do as you wish. Your guides will pack your things and close your quarters. You can meet in front of the castle for the ride to the airport."

"What about Bailey and my car?" Kim asked.

"Bailey's right here. Your car will be at the airport." Danielle left.

The women sat in silence.

Finally, Kim stood. "I feel like someone died. Since I doubt that's what Julia wants us to feel, I'm going on a hike, enjoy the last few hours here, and celebrate this weekend. Would anyone care to go? I know a quiet beach not too far."

"I thought of going to the casino," Marge admitted, "but, maybe I'll come with you instead. I could use some time for thinking, too. Besides, I'm afraid to let any of you out of my sight."

Kate looked at Denise. "What do you feel like doing?"

"I'm not much of a hiker, but, if it's not too far, I'd like for all of us to be together."

Kate waved her arm. "It's unanimous. We'll go to the beach. It'll be fun to spend the last part of our weekend together."

When they arrived at the beach, they all found comfortable places to stretch out. Bailey ran in and out of the water, splashing everything in sight.

"Finding out about Julia and this castle may be harder than I thought," Kate pointed out. "I hope she doesn't stop me."

"Would she?" Denise asked.

"I don't know. At least she isn't going to stop us from keeping in touch with one another. I hope we do."

"Why wouldn't we?" Marge asked.

"We don't live close," Kim replied, "and, we don't have much in common besides this weekend. It would be easy to drift apart and get caught up in our own lives, especially after we celebrate our birthdays."

"I'll take it upon myself to make sure we stay in touch," Denise said. "Anyone who doesn't cooperate will pay."

Marge took off her clothes and joined Bailey in the lake. She immediately came up for air and shouted, "Christ, this water's cold! Wow!"

"It's so nice and peaceful here, except for Marge shouting," Denise said. "I should've brought my book to read. I'm almost finished with it."

"What is it?" Kate asked.

"A Woman's Worth."

"Is it any good?"

"I didn't think so until this weekend, but it fits with what's happened here. I'll finish it before we get to Dallas and loan it to you."

"Great."

CHAPTER TWENTY-SIX

The limousine arrived at the castle, and Hildy bounded out. Hi, gals. How was the weekend?"

"The best," Denise answered.

"Great. All your things are at the airport and ready to go. You car's at the airport, Kim."

"What about Bailey? You don't want him riding in your limo, do you?"

"Sure. He can hop in the front seat with me," Hildy laughed.

"He'll love that."

"Where are our guides?" Marge asked. "I wanted to say goodbye."

"They'll be at the airport to see you off," Hildy replied.

After taking one last, long look at the castle, they got into the limousine. They secretly hoped for a glimpse of Julia, but she didn't appear.

"We didn't see much of Hildy this weekend," Denise said.

"Maybe she doesn't work for Julia," Kate noted. "Hildy, where have you been all weekend? Don't you work for Julia?"

"You think all I do is drive her guests around? I have a business to run," Hildy replied.

Kate glanced at Kim. "This is your limo service?"

"Yes."

"What do you call it?" Kate asked.

"Hildy's. What else?"

Kate whispered, "Her license plate is H Limo. That should be easy to track down."

"Does Julia have these conferences often?" Denise asked.

"I wouldn't know. This is the first time I've been out here."

Kate was shocked. "You never saw the castle before?"

"Never."

"How long have you lived in Tahoe?"

"About a week."

"How'd Julia find you?"

"Probably the same way she found you."

When they arrived at the airport, the jet was waiting at the end of the runway. Kim's car was parked next to it. The pilot and the personal guides waved as the limousine drove up.

Kate jumped out as soon as the limo stopped. She quickly wrote something in her notepad.

"What are you doing?" Kim asked.

"Writing down the limo's license plate number and the tail numbers on the plane. Maybe they'll trace back to Julia. Who knows? They both might belong to Julia. I'll need all the information I can find to solve this mystery."

Kim laughed. "You make it sound so cloak-and-dagger."

Kate's eyes narrowed, "It might be. There are too many un-answered questions here."

Everyone said good-bye, and the personal guides joined in for a group hug. They hung on tightly, not wanting to let go. They promised to keep in touch.

The guides walked slowly to the limousine and left with Hildy, waving frantically out the windows. Kate, Denise and Marge boarded the plane.

Kim watched the plane taxi down the runway. She and Bailey walked toward the car. The limousine was gone, and when she turned, so was the plane. She shrugged and opened the car door.

"Well, Bailey," she said, snapping her seat belt. "The weekend's over, but what a weekend. Do you have any idea what we've been through?"

He cocked his head from his place in the back seat, then settled down on a blanket Karen had laid out for him. Kim glanced at her watch. The second hand was moving again—it was 3:02.

She chuckled, "Marge must be happy now. She finally knows what time it is."

She drove home feeling happy. She had a good idea what she was going to do for her fiftieth birthday, and renewed hope of getting her family back together. She was calm and at peace with herself. It was a great feeling.

In some ways, she felt as if she'd been away for weeks, relaxing at a castle she never knew existed. In all the times she'd been to Tahoe and hiked around the lake, she never saw the castle and never heard anyone talk about it. She knew she'd never miss it again.

Suddenly, she felt hot. She broke into a sweat and felt like tearing off her clothes. Her back, pressed against the car seat, felt on fire. She rolled down the window, but the cool air had little effect.

As quickly as it began, it stopped. Kim grinned and said, "By Georgette, I just had my first hot flash."

Something about it pleased her, but she was also apprehensive about whether hot flashes and menopause would interfere with her life.

Kim parked on the street in front of her house. As she bounced out of the car, she looked upward. "Thanks, Julia. I know you arranged this spot for me."

She and Bailey ran up the stairs without carrying anything in. The door was unlocked.

"Linda, are you here?" she called. "We're back from the castle."

Linda ran into the hall. "What, no, 'Honey, I'm home?'" She threw her arms around Kim and patted Bailey's head. He stood patiently between the two women.

"I know how you hate it," Kim said shyly.

"You should go away more often. I like the little changes. So, how was it? Come in and tell me everything."

"I had my first hot flash," Kim blurted. "At least, I think it was a hot flash. Either that, or I'm coming down with something. It was weird. It happened in the car on my way home. It was like...."

"Wait a minute. You've been gone for three days. I haven't heard a word from you. You go to a mysterious castle at Lake Tahoe, and all you want to talk about is a hot flash? I know about those. Tell me about the castle."

They laughed so hard they fell down. Bailey came over and licked their faces.

Kim gasped for air, "It does sound a little silly, doesn't it? It was the last thing that happened in an otherwise strange weekend, and, well, you know...."

"No, I don't. Tell me. Come into the kitchen. I've got dinner in the oven. We can talk there. What's that around your neck?"

"Oh," Kim held the necklace. "Let me get my things, then we'll get comfortable. This will take some time to explain."

During dinner, Kim related everything that happened at the castle, including how their watches stopped. She checked hers again to make sure it was still running. She told Linda about the other women and how Marge had bought necklaces for everyone. She brought out her copy of the rite of passage they developed.

"I shot four rolls of film. Wait til you see the other women, and the castle. You won't believe my campsite."

Linda thumbed through the folder. "You all came up with ideas?"

"We sure did. Don't you like my idea about the houseboat at Lake Shasta?"

"I suppose, but how are you going to get everyone there?"

Kim wrinkled her brow. "That's the hard part. It was easy to decide on the houseboat. Then, it hit me. I'll have contest winner announcements printed and send them to everyone. It's kind of like what Julia did to us. They'll be told they won a three-day, two-night, all-expense-paid vacation on a houseboat the last weekend in July."

"Will anyone fall for that?"

"They have to. I have faith it'll work out."

"Who'll you invite?"

"My folks, Anna and John, Joy and Kathy, Lori and Rebecca, Ralph and Patti, Ron and Becky, and C and J."

"Your folks?"

"It's worth a try."

"All those people on one houseboat?"

Kim smiled, "Okay, I'll rent two."

"That'll be expensive."

"Maybe this is what I've been saving for. I'm worth it, and I want to get my family back together. There are details to work out, and there isn't much time, but I'm going for it."

"If you need any help, let me know."

"Thanks. I need your support."

"What about your folks?"

"What do you mean?"

"There's a good chance they won't go. If they do, they might leave when they see me."

Kim sighed, "Perhaps. It's a chance I have to take. Hopefully, they'll think leaving will look bad."

"Are you sure you weren't at a power-of-positive-thinking conference?"

"That might be another word for it, but it was more like a women's power conference. If that old lady can do what she did in one weekend, I can handle a small miracle."

"Who is she?"

"We don't know, but Kate intends to find out."

"I think you're crazy, but I'm glad you're going to do it. I hope you won't be disappointed."

"No matter what happens, I won't be disappointed, because this celebration is for me. I'll be doing what I want to do, and those who love and care for me will be there."

"Which weekend was that?" Linda joked. "I have to check my social calendar."

That night when they crawled into bed, Kim was so excited, she didn't know if she'd be able to sleep. There were so many things on her mind. She had to start preparations the next day.

Kim snuggled up to Linda. "I'm glad to be home."

"Me, too. I missed you."

"Do you believe in guardian angels?"

"You mean like alter egos?" Linda asked sleepily, "a voice from within, like your conscience?"

"Something like that."

"Sure."

"Have you ever met yours?"

"I don't think your conscience is something you can meet."

"I met mine at the conference."

As Linda drifted off to sleep, she mumbled, "That's nice. I'm happy for you."

"Her name is Karen."

CHAPTER TWENTY-SEVEN

Ronald was waiting when Kate's jet landed in New York. He walked slowly toward the plane. As soon as he saw Kate deplane, he started running.

"Kate!" he waved.

She waved and waited until he caught up with her, then she hugged him. "I'm glad to see you."

"I missed you. Did you have a good time? Let me help with your bags."

"You sure can. Ronald, this is Jan, our pilot. Jan, my husband, Ronald."

"Pleased to meet you." Jan shook his hand.

"Where do you go next?" Kate asked.

"This is it. I get to go home until my next assignment."

"Where's home?"

"Wherever I put this baby down," Jan called as she climbed back into the plane.

"Thanks for a wonderful flight. I never had a smoother ride."

"Probably not," she grinned, closing the door.

"When did you leave Tahoe?" Ronald asked.

"Hey, wait!" Kate turned back toward the plane, but it was gone. "How the hell could she disappear to quickly?"

"What's wrong?" Ronald queried.

"There's something odd here. It's still light." She looked at her watch. It read 6:02.

"What's going on, Kate?"

"I don't know. It's the damndest thing. All our watches stopped when we arrived in Tahoe."

"Everyone's?"

"Yes. All the time we were there the clocks read three o'clock. When we left this afternoon, Marge looked at her watch and said it was working again."

"Marge who?"

"Honey, please. I'll tell you all about it. Pay attention to this. As we took off, our watches read two minutes after three. That would've made it two minutes after six here. When we landed, my watch showed two minutes after six."

"What did you have to drink on that plane?"

She slapped his shoulder. "Nothing, you fool. I know I shouldn't be surprised by anything after the weekend we had, but the timing doesn't make sense. We made stops in Dallas and Minot, too."

"Maybe it really wasn't three when you left Tahoe."

"That's possible, knowing some of the things we've been through, but it was mid-afternoon, three hours difference, and at least a five hour flight with the stops," Kate reasoned. "I'd almost venture a guess that everyone got home at six o'clock her time, even Kim. Cute move, Julia. How'd you do it?"

Ronald eyed her inquisitively.

"Never mind. I'll tell you all about it on the way home."

"We don't live together anymore," he reminded her.

Kate leaned over and kissed his cheek. "I missed you a lot while I was away. I missed your stability and ability to carry on a decent conversation. I missed the comfort we've had all these years. I missed your humor, and even your body a few times. If you're willing, I'd like to try again."

He beamed and drove home as quickly as he could. Kate explained all the details of the weekend, emphasizing the peculiar things that happened.

That night, in bed, Ronald admitted, "Im not sure what to make of your weekend, Kate. It sounds pretty mysterious."

"It was. It was also the greatest experience I ever had. None of it seemed real, yet we dealt with real problems. I feel like I got in touch with myself, and I may have met my guardian angel in the process."

Ronald started to speak, but she covered his mouth with her hand.

"Don't say anything, please. With a few minor changes, I could be exactly where I want to be in life," she continued.

"Changes?"

"Yes. What would you say if I said I was considering selling my partnership in the law firm?"

He sat straight up. "Jesus, Kate! You said minor changes."

"Okay, maybe a few major ones, too. I've been wanting to do something different with my life for a while."

"I didn't know that."

"I haven't verbalized it. But, I've been thinking I could use the money from the firm to open a Liz Claiborne shop in the center."

"How long have you been thinking about this?"

"Two years. This weekend finally gave me the courage to try. After what I've been through this weekend, this will be easy. It's not like putting a fifteen-story penthouse in a three-story building."

They laughed and started wrestling in bed.

"I'll support your decision anyway I can," Ronald said.

"Don't be silly. You don't wear Liz' clothes."

"Maybe she could start making men's clothes."

"Actually, I think she does."

"I'll wait until you open your store before I buy any."

"Before I can do any of this, however, I've got some investigating to do. Maybe you can help me. You have a better investigator than I do."

"Investigate what?"

"We decided I was going to find out about Julia, the castle, the whole mystery surrounding this conference."

"You can't just accept what happened for what it was?"

"No. We don't know what happened. We need closure."

"Got anything to work with?"

"Not much. The woman who hosted the conference was Julia Worthington."

"Married name?"

"Don't know."

"Anything else?"

"She was born on July 31, 1895 at nine thirty-five in the morning in California."

"For crying out loud! Why don't you make it difficult?"

"I've got more. The limousine service she used is owned by a woman named Hildy, and she just started her business. I have the personalized plate from the limo. I have the address, phone number and fax number for the castle."

"That might help."

"Then there's the plane. We could check with the airports to see who filed flight plans. I have the plane's tail numbers."

"That's all?"

"What do you mean? That's a lot of information. Your investigator has come up with plenty on less. This woman's one hundred years old. She must've left an extensive paper trail. Kim has her picture, too. She stood with us one night, and Kim's guide snapped a picture of all of us. Come on. Aren't you even a little intrigued?"

"Yes, but are you certain you want to find out the answers?"

"Of course. Why do you ask?"

"I'm not sure. It sounds like one of those things on the edge of time or reality. It's a Twilight Zone thing that maybe didn't happen. It might be best left undiscovered."

"Right, like four menopausal women got together, went crazy simultaneously, and made it all up? I don't think so. We're planning a reunion after we celebrate our fiftieth birthdays, and I want some information to share with everyone. Will you help me?"

"Of course. We'll start tomorrow. Have you settled on your birthday plans?"

"The first thing I'll do is publish a legal notice in the paper."

"What kind of legal notice?"

"I haven't worded it yet, but it'll be along the lines of ones they use to announce readings and fictitious name announcements. It's something to declare I'm of sound mind and body and am entering into true womanhood."

"Why not make it like a wedding announcement, complete with a picture?"

"I've been thinking about that. Don't you think it's a little decadent?"

"It's either decandent or it's not. There's no such thing as a little decadent."

"It won't make me sound vain?"

"If you don't toot your own horn, who will?"

"Good point," she laughed. "Do you think the Times will run it?"

He put his arms around her. "Honey, I thought this entrance into womanhood was something you were proud of. Isn't that why you went to the conference?"

"Well, yes...."

"Imagine someone seeing your picture and announcement and thinking it was a good idea. She might do it, too. Pretty soon, we'd have a whole city of women who are proud of themselves. It's better to have your life story in the paper when you're fifty, instead of when you're dead."

Kate swatted at him and missed. "I get the point. I'll do it. Maybe I can get a plug in for my new shop."

"You women stop at nothing."

"If I'm paying for it, I'll add the plug."

"Now that we have that settled, can we get some sleep?"

"I'm not through."

"Why did I know that?" he moaned.

"I want to throw a reception at the house. People can drop by between two and five to wish me well."

"That's a fun idea. Want them to bring gifts?"

"Of course."

"I can help with the planning," Ronald offered. "We'll need drinks and food. I'll get some prices from the caterers."

"Great, and make sure they'll clean up. Neither of us should have to do it."

"I'll help pay for it."

"Heavens, no. I won't hear of it. This is my party. I should have plenty from the sale of my partnership for my new shop and the party. After all, I only turn fifty once."

He sighed, "Thank God."

CHAPTER TWENTY-EIGHT

As soon as Marge's watch started working again, she began planning her fiftieth birthday party. She wanted the biggest bash Minot ever saw.

Marge was the first to leave the plane. She hastily hugged Kate and Denise and promised to write. She waved good-bye, struggling with her luggage, as she walked for the terminal.

She laughed when she saw Greg run into the building, late as usual.

"Hi, Sweetie," he panted. "Thought I'd be late."

"You are. What's new?"

He kissed her cheek and reached for her bags. "How was the trip?"

"Great. You should've seen the penthouse I had. It was a beautiful suite, with a pool, entrance to a casino, and...."

She stopped, not wanting to tell him too much. He wouldn't understand, especially the odd parts.

"Did you solve all the problems of women?"

"It wasn't that kind of conference. It was...more of a personal thing."

"In other words, you don't want to talk about it?"

"That's not it. Well, there are some things I'd rather not talk about."

"Oaky. Tell me what you want. Were there lots of other women there? Did you get anything resolved for yourself?"

"Yes, there were other women. I've decided to throw a huge party to celebrate turning fifty."

"Good. I'll help."

"That's sweet, Greg, but this is something I have to do alone. I don't need any help."

He was crushed. "Come on, Marge. I wasn't trying to horn in. I just want to help."

"Don't worry. You'll be invited. Hell the whole town will be invited. This is my thing. I don't want to miss any of the fun."

"What about us? Did you make any decisions? Will you marry me?"

Marge was impatient. "I'm still married, Greg. I have to deal with that before I think of anyone else. I don't want to hurt your feelings, but this isn't about us, it's about me."

"But, I love you. I don't want to lose you. Where do I fit in?"

"I don't know. I need time to figure things out."

"How long will that take?"

"Greg, I don't know," she shouted. "I don't want to think about it. I have less than two months to get the party going. Give me some space."

They drove to the house in silence. Finally, he asked, "Will you spend the night with me?"

"No. I'm not in the mood. I want to go home."

"When will I see you?"

"I don't know. I'll call."

The drive home seemed shorter than usual. She was anxious to see Lobo, but didn't look forward to dealing with Walter. She didn't love him anymore, but was used to having him around. She thought of him more as a brother, but didn't think he'd want to hear that.

When she arrived, Walter was sitting out front with Lobo.

"Just great," she said. "He's using Lobo to get to me. He doesn't like my dog."

Marge parked and Lobo bounded across the yard to her. She got out and hugged him. "Lobo, it's good to see you. I missed you."

Walter walked up and held his arms out. "Did you miss me, too?"

Marge was angry, but couldn't say why. She reached for a suitcase. "Yes, Walter."

They walked toward the house with her things.

"How was the weekend? Did you enjoy yourself?"

"I had a wonderful time, but I don't feel like talking about it now."

"You must be tired."

"I'm not," Marge insisted. "It was one of the most relaxing vacations I ever had. I've got a lot on my mind, and most of what happened this weekend doesn't concern you. You wouldn't understand."

"Understand? Or, is it that you don't want to tell me?" he snapped. "In case you hadn't noticed, everything you do concerns me."

"Walter, please leave me alone."

"We have to talk. I can't go on like this, and I don't think you're happy with the way things are between us either. I moved back into the house. I want to get on with our marriage."

Marge glared at him. "Fine. You can have the house. I'll move out back. I need time and space. I don't want to talk about anything now."

Walter protested, but Marge moved into the guest house. Lobo was thrilled. That meant he could sleep on the bed.

The first week Marge was home, she isolated herself from everyone. She avoided Walter and didn't call Greg. She plunged into a remodeling job and hired two helpers for the heavy work. It felt good to be working.

At the end of each day, she closed the door to her small cottage and dreamed about the penthouse at Lake Tahoe. She would drink beer and talk to Lobo for hours before quietly passing out on the couch.

Marge was ecstatic when she learned she could rent the VFW Hall for only $300. She booked it for nine o'clock in the evening, Saturday, July 29. When the hall manager told her she could have it as long as she liked, she invited him. His only stipulation was that the hall had to be cleaned by noon Sunday.

With the location firm, she immediately called Timmy Bowen.

"Timmy? Marge Sinclair."

"Hi, Marge. How are you?"

"Fine, thanks. The reason I called is I'm going to have a big fiftieth birthday party on July twenty-ninth."

"Oh? Who for?"

"Me, you idiot."

"You're gonna be fifty?"

"Yes."

"You sure don't look it, and you sure as hell don't act like it." He laughed.

"Thanks. Anyway, I was wondering if your group's still together."

"The shitkickers?"

"Yeah. Is there another one?"

"No. We haven't played for a while, but we're together."

"Would you play for the party?"

"Yeah, but it'll cost you."

"How much?"

"Two hundred for the whole group."

Marge smiled. They weren't real good, but the price was right. "The party starts at nine, and I might want you to play into the early morning if people keep partying."

"It's another fifty if we play past midnight."

"How about if I throw in all the beer you can drink?"

"Hell, forget the extra fifty. We'll drink more than that. We'll start practicing this week."

"Great. I want lots of shit-kicking music."

"You got it, Lady. Can't believe you're gonna be fifty."

Things were lining up well. Marge submitted an ad in the local paper, inviting everyone in town. Food and music would be free, but beer would cost a dollar a glass.

She called Ginny at the You Name It catering service. "Ginny? This is Marge Sinclair."

"Hi, Marge. How's it going? I heard you're planning a big bash for your fiftieth."

"How'd you know? The ad's not out yet."

"Greg told me the other night at Dino's."

"I was wondering if you'd cater it. It's the 29th of July at the VFW Hall."

"How many people?"

"I'm not sure. The ad invites everyone in town."

"You might have several hundred people."

"I hope so."

"How long will this thing last?"

"We're starting at nine and hoping to go until the wee hours."

"How long do want the food out?"

"At least until midnight, maybe later."

Ginny whistled. "This will cost a bundle."

"I'll only be fifty once."

"What kind of food do you want?"

"Any suggestions?"

"For that many people, I'd keep it simple. Maybe some veggies, chips, dip, sandwich fixings, and a hot dish or two like chicken wings or meatballs."

"That sounds great. Can you do it?"

"Sure, but it'll cost."

"How much?"

Ginny calculated over the phone. "Say two hundred people and enough food for five hours. It might run as high as six hundred dollars."

"Sold. Book it. Can I hire you to clean up afterward?"

"For another hundred."

"I'll take it."

That night, Marge munched on a tuna sandwich and drank a beer. Everything was falling into place. Lobo sat faithfully at her side, waiting for tidbits to fall. The only thing left was to arrange for the beer. She would call Fred at Smith's Distributing. They handled Michelob, and he'd give her a good deal. She'd see if Bill and Gene, the day bartenders at Dino's, would work that night.

There was a soft knock on the door. Lobo looked up and growled softly.

"It's okay, Lobo." Marge patted his head. "Who's there?"

"Walter. Can I come in?"

""I suppose, but make it quick. I'm going to bed in a few minutes."

Walter walked in and was appalled by the mess. "Christ! When was the last time you cleaned in here?"

"What do you want?"

"This place looks like a pig sty. There are empty bottles everywhere, and you let Lobo in."

"What the hell do you want, Walter?" she demanded.

"I wanted to talk, but I don't think this is a good time. You're obviously drunk."

Marge stood. "I'm not drunk. I've had two beers. Now, if you have something to say, say it and leave."

"First, your friend Kate, from New York called and wants you to call her back as soon as possible. Denise has called several times and wants to know why you're not returning her calls."

"Is that it?"

"No. There's one more thing. I've been going to some meetings, and I would like you to come with me."

"What?"

"Marge, you're drinking too much. This group is good. I'd like you to come to an Alcoholics Anonymous meeting with me. You need help, and...."

"Get the hell out of here. You know shit. So what if I drink a few beers now and then? I work hard all day, I deserve to relax with a beer or two. It's no big deal, and I sure as hell ain't an alcoholic. I can handle my beer. If you think I'm an alcoholic, then you're the one with the problem, not me. Go to your damn meeting by yourself, if it makes you feel better. Leave me alone."

"Marge, calm down and take a look at yourself. This place is a mess. You're a mess. Just go once and listen to what they have to say, please?" Walter begged.

"Get the fuck out, Walter," Marge screamed at him.

Walter slammed the door on his way out. Lobo barked at him.

"That's right, Lobo, you tell 'em." Marge got another beer from the refrigerator.

"I don't drink that much. He's just trying to think of something that I'll do with him. He's pissed because I won't go back to him."

CHAPTER TWENTY-NINE

Droves of people came through the doors of the hall the night of the party. Marge couldn't believe how many people showed up. Most of them she didn't know, but it didn't bother her. They came to help her celebrate.

As people came in, Marge's friends sold tickets for a dollar each. They could be exchanged for a large plastic mug of Michelob at one of three kegs placed around the ballroom.

"Marge," Kelly said, "if we keep selling tickets like this, you'll pay for this bash. You might even make a profit."

"Paying for the party's good enough. Who are all these people?"

"We have no idea. Many of them said they came because they wanted to meet the woman with guts enough to announce she's fifty. Some women said they wished they'd thought of this."

"Did you see the gift table?" Carol asked.

"Gift table?"

"Yeah. Kelly and I had to set up a table. Everyone's bringing something."

Marge looked at the table. It was stacked high with presents. For a brief moment, she thought about Julia, Kim, Kate and Denise. She wished she had invited them. She was so wrapped up in herself, she forgot.

The celebrating started early when Kelly, Carol and Marge finished with the decorations. Marge painted a large banner that draped over the dance floor—*The second half of my life will be better than the first.* Black and red crepe paper streamers hung everywhere. Marge said the black ones represented mourning for her first fifty years, and the red ones were for new life in the second fifty.

Timmy and the Shitkickers were setting up and tuning their instruments. Ginny and her crew finished stocking tables with plates of goodies.

When Marge walked toward the food, she saw Greg carrying trays from the kitchen.

"Hi, Greg," Marge said nervously/ "I'm glad you made it to the party."

"Hi," he replied coolly. "I'm here helping Ginny. Looks like a great party."

Marge didn't know what to say next. She hadn't spoken to Greg since her return from Lake Tahoe. Before she could open her mouth, Ginny came by.

"When you're through with the veggies, Honey, would you help Pat with the chicken? Thanks." Ginny patted his shoulder.

Greg nodded and looked at Marge.

"Honey?" she asked.

"Well...Ginny and I have been going out for a while."

Marge was shocked. "I didn't know. Are you in love with her?"

"I think so."

"Great. I hope you two are happy." She walked off in a daze. Just because she hadn't called him in a few weeks was no reason to fall in love with someone else.

"He must not have cared that much about me." She filled her

cup again as she walked past a keg near the bandstand.

The party was a resounding success. The band was good, and people danced. Marge was dancing with men she'd never seen before.

At one point, Greg asked her to dance. "I owe you an explanation."

"No, you don't," she insisted.

"It's just that I realized you didn't love me. When you didn't call, I decided to stop feeling sorry for myself and get on with my life."

"You don't have to explain, Greg. I understand. It's better this way."

"Are you still with Walter? I haven't seen him tonight."

Marge froze. She forgot to invite Walter. In all her preparations, she never mentioned the party to him. He probably wouldn't come, anyway. Besides, he probably saw the ad.

Marge looked at Greg. "To be honest, I didn't invite him. I've been living in the guest house. We hardly speak. He's on a crusade to get me into Alcoholics Anonymous."

"Sorry. I assumed you two worked things out." He glanced at the beer in her hand. "You have been known to put a few of those away."

"For Christ's sake, Greg, don't you start. Get off my back. This is my birthday. I'm entitled to have a few too many if I want."

They finished their dance and Greg returned to the kitchen. Marge saw him one more time that evening, dancing cheek-to-cheek with Ginny.

Marge lost track of time. She knew she had too much to drink, but if she stopped, the hangover would start that much sooner, so she kept on.

Some of the people were starting to leave when Walter walked in. He looked nice—clean-shaven and dressed in a blue and red checked shirt with a black scarf around his neck. She couldn't remember the last time she saw him look so good.

"Walter, how good of you to come. You look great. Maybe we should...."

He gently took her hand. "Don't say anything. I didn't come to party. I came to wish you a happy birthday and tell you I'm leaving. I took a job with a construction company in Missoula."

"What?"

"We both know it's over."

"That may be, but I don't see why you have to pack up and leave so suddenly."

"It's not sudden. I've been trying to talk to you for weeks. I have to go. I can't stay and watch you destroy yourself."

"What the hell are you talking about?"

"Your drinking. It's...."

"Jesus Christ!" she shouted. "Just because I have a beer or two on occasion, you think I'm an alcoholic. Maybe you should go. I can do better without you."

Walter turned to walk away, then stopped. "I'm sorry it had to end like this. I wish you the best."

"Get the hell out of here!"

Walter left.

Marge remembered nothing after that. When she woke the next day, she lay on a lumpy, uncomfortable sofa in the ladies' room at the VFW hall. Her head spun, and she couldn't seem to focus her eyes. When she sat up, she was sick to her stomach. Her mouth was stuffed with cotton.

As she staggered to her feet, Marge glanced in the mirror. Her hair was a mess, her clothes were crumpled. She looked at her watch. It was ten. She assumed that wasn't ten in the evening.

Marge wandered into the ballroom. Ginny, Greg, and two others were cleaning.

"Hi, Marge," Ginny greeted. "How are you?"

Marge groaned.

"You passed out about three, so we put you on the sofa. We didn't know what else to do. We closed the party after that. We went home and slept for a while before trying to clean this place. Your presents are loaded in your car. What a haul. We tried to leave room for you," Ginny joked.

"Thanks. I appreciate it. Do you need me?"

"No. We're almost done. Why don't you go home?"

Marge looked around. "I just might do that. I know I partied too much, but I'll never be fifty again. I'm sure I had a wonderful time."

When she pulled into the driveway, Walter's truck and trailer were gone. She was glad. She hated having that parked in the front yard. It was one of his homemade jobs—half primed, half painted. It looked terrible.

She vaguely remembered what he told her at the party. She couldn't believe he'd leave without talking to her first.

Lobo ran out to greet her. She hugged him. "Thank God you're still here. You wouldn't leave me, would you? Did you help Walter pack?"

She opened the front door. "Ah, we have the house back."

Lobo followed her in. The house was so clean it almost sparkled.

"I never saw this place look so good." She walked past the dining room table and saw a bouquet of flowers. Beside them was a note and present.

She sat at the table. Lobo plopped on the floor next to her. The flowers were fresh and beautiful. She read the note.

Happy Birthday, Marge. The
flowers and present are for you.
I'll be at Granite Construction
in Missoula, if you need to reach
me. I wish you well and hope you
realize you need help.

Love, Walter

She unwrapped the present. It was a book, "My Name is Bill." It was about alcoholism. She threw it across the room. Lobo crawled under the table. She decided to take a nap and open her presents later.

Marge didn't feel much better after her nap. She went to the refrigerator for a beer, but there weren't any, so she stumbled to the guest house. That refrigerator was empty, too. The cottage was a mess. She didn't remember leaving it like that. She closed the door, promising to clean it later.

Unsure what to do, Marge took Lobo for a hike. He was thrilled. They headed down the fence and through the pasture. After walking along the road, they came to the cutoff for the creek. Walking next to Winding Creek always made her feel better. Lobo romped and played like a puppy, picking up sticks and bringing them to Marge to throw.

"You know, maybe I have been drinking too much, but who can blame me with everything that's happened? I can stop if I want. Maybe I will. Heaven knows, I had enough last night to last a lifetime. At fifty, I should be more responsible. I have my business to attend to. Walter and Greg are gone, so it's just us. Maybe things will look up."

On the way back, she decided to call the women from the Tahoe conference.

"They'll be celebrating this weekend, too. I'll call and wish them a happy birthday. I haven't kept in touch."

When she returned home, she called Kim first.

"Hi, you've reached the home of Kim, Linda, and Bailey. Sorry we can't come to the phone right now, but, if you'll leave your name and number, we'll get back to you as soon as possible."

There was a loud beep.

"Hi, Kim, this is Marge. You're probably out on the houseboat this weekend. Hope it's going well. Had my bash last night—what a doozy. Just wanted to wish you a happy birthday. I hope we can get together soon. I'd like to go back to the castle. I think I missed some of the messages we were supposed to get. Have a good day and call me."

Marge went to the kitchen for a glass of water. She knew she'd probably get answering machines at Kate and Denise's, but she decided to try. Sure enough, Denise had her machine on.

"Hi, Denise. It's Marge wishing you a happy birthday. I'm a little hung over from my celebration, but it was better than I could've hoped. Have a good day and call me when you get home."

She dialed Kate, ready to leave another message.

"Hello?" Kate answered.

"Kate? Is that you?"

"Marge?"

"Yes."

"Where the hell have you been?"

"What do you mean? I'm right here."

"We've been trying to reach you for weeks."

"Really?"

"Yes. Didn't Walter tell you we called? He said he would. I even sent a telegram. Denise wrote at least one letter, too."

Marge was silent. She never went into the main house, even

for her mail. "Well, I...Walter and I.... I moved out for a while."

"Why didn't you let us know? We were worried about you."

"Sorry. I was wrapped up in my troubles and my party. I let things go."

"Apology accepted. I'm happy to hear from you. Are you all right?"

"I'm not sure. Greg has a new girlfriend, and Walter moved to Montana. I think I've been drinking a little too much. I was thinking of calling Julia. I feel like I missed something at the conference."

Kate laughed. "Don't even bother. None of us have been able to reach her or the castle, and we've uncovered a lot of strange things associated with Julia."

Marge was intrigued, "Like what?"

"I can't go into all the details now, because my rite of passage reception is just starting. Listen, we're thinking of going back to the castle the weekend after Labor Day, interested?"

"Sure."

"I'm setting up a conference call tomorrow, at, let's see, six your time. We can make plans."

"Great," Marge sighed. "I want to go back. I need help. And, I want to see you all again."

"We'll call tomorrow."

"Thanks. Have a wonderful rite of passage."

CHAPTER THIRTY

Denise was happy to be back in Dallas. Gene met her at the airport and she ran to embrace him. For the first time in years, she was happy to see a man.

"How was your trip?"

"Marvelous."

"Can I help with the luggage?"

Denise turned back. "Heavens, I almost forgot my things." She walked back toward the plane as Jan finished unloading her bags. "I'm sorry. I meant to help with those."

"No problem. Looks like you had better things to do."

Denise blushed. "Jan, this is Gene. Gene, Jan."

"Pleased to met you, Ma'am." He nodded and tipped his hat.

Kate stuck her head out the door. "Hey, Denise. Is that the hunk you told us about?"

"Pay no attention," Denise explained, "she's joking. Get out here, Kate."

Gene sauntered to Kate and said, "Yes, I'm the hunk. Who might you be?"

"Great sense of humor, Denise," Kate shouted. "That's a good sign." She held out her hand. "Hi. I'm Kate. I'm the good-looking black woman she'll be telling you about."

"For crying out loud, Kate," Denise said, "you were the only African-American woman there."

"You forgot Kathy."

Denise smiled, "She doesn't count. She was merely an extension of you. Anyway, she was too young to be included."

They waved good-bye. Denise already missed her new friends.

On the drive home, Gene said, "Okay, tell me all about it. Don't leave out anything. You look wonderful. It must've been a restful vacation."

"Oh, it was," she cooed. "It was the most wonderful thing that ever happened to me. I don't understand everything that happened, but I feel like a new woman. I feel alive and important."

He glanced at her. "You do seem different—more positive and assertive."

"I am. I'm thrilled to be turning fifty, and I intend to make some changes in my life."

"Where do I fit in?" he asked.

"You're a big part of it. I did a lot of thinking. I care for you a great deal—no, I love you. I've been ignoring my own feelings. If you still want me, I'd be happy to marry you. I want to spend the rest of my life with you."

Gene was shocked. "You'll marry me? Oh, Denise, I'm so happy? When?"

"Don't rush me. I have some things I need to do first, and we have some things to talk about, but I was thinking maybe sometime around the first of the year."

"I don't know if I can wait that long, but it's more than I hoped for, so I'll take it. How about New Year's Day?"

"Why not New Year's Eve?"

"Even better. One less day to wait."

Denise explained, "That way, we'll start out the new year already married, and it would give us some tax breaks for this year."

He smiled. "I love that about you. You can combine business with pleasure and they both come out better. What's this stuff you need to do?"

"I want to start a nonprofit organization to help women with their rite of passage. I want to design plaques to be presented to these women. Any woman will be able to get one by contacting the organization."

"Do you have a name for this group?"

"I've been toying with Passage of Women Ever-Reaching, or POWER. What do you think?"

"I like it, but as long as it appeals to women, that's important. How will you run this?"

"First, I'll file papers to form the corporation, then I'll solicit donations from local groups—maybe a few national ones, too. I might even try for a government grant."

"How do you fit into all this?"

She giggled, "I'll be the executive director. I'd draw a salary, and I might be able to hire some help if needed. Of course, we'd need lots of volunteers. We would sponsor ceremonies to present the plaques. We could send speakers all over the country, educating women about what to expect when they reach fifty and go through menopause. Who knows? The possibilities are unlimited."

"It sounds time-consuming," Gene pointed out. "How can you do this and hold down a job?"

"I won't."

Gene blinked. "You're giving up your job?"

"Yes. I can still do some tax work on the side, if I need more income, and I could help you with the restaurant books, too."

Gene beamed. "You mean restaurants."

"Oh, how insensitive of me. Did you get the other one open?"

"The grand opening is set for Thursday. I didn't want to open it without you. Will you accompany me?"

"I'd be honored. That's exciting, Gene."

When he pulled into Denise's driveway, she said, "Come in. I've been saving a bottle of Chardonnay for a special occasion and this is it."

Gene opened the car door and then reached into the glove box. He slipped something into his pocket.

"What's that?"

"Nothing."

She tickled him and tried to reach into his pocket. "Come on, what is it?"

"Okay. I bought this some time ago, but never knew if I'd be able to give it to you."

He handed her a small jewelry box. She opened it and found a beautiful diamond ring. "How'd you know I would say yes?"

"Wishful thinking." He gave her a bear hug and lifted her off her feet.

Denise slipped the ring on and they went inside. She poured two glasses of wine and joined Gene on the couch.

"To us," she toasted.

"I'll drink to that."

"Gene, there are several things we need to discuss before we get married."

"Such as?"

"Where will we live?"

He became somber. "I hadn't thought about it. I assumed we'd live in my house. It's bigger, and I doubt my stuff would fit in yours."

"That may be true, but that was your home with Gloria. I wouldn't feel comfortable."

"I never thought about that."

"We don't have to decide tonight, but think about it. What

about a honeymoon? Will we have one? Where will we go? What kind of ceremony do we want? Who do we invite?"

"I guess we do have a lot to talk about."

"There's more. You're going to have to deal with my going through menopause, and what about my new organization, and...."

"Wait! We have time to work those things out. Let's start with something easier."

"Like what?"

"Like how much we love each other."

She nodded and whispered, "I love you, Gene." She leaned over and kissed him long and deeply.

"That's better." He kissed her in return.

CHAPTER THIRTY-ONE

Denise worked hard in the following weeks. At Gene's grand opening of his second restaurant, he introduced her as his fiancee, and donated ten thousand dollars to her new foundation.

She approached other businessmen and women who pledged donations once she filed the articles of incorporation for POWER. Her accounting firm, which wasn't happy to lose her, made a donation, too.

When Denise arrived home one day, Gene's car was in the driveway. She walked quickly into the house.

"Gene, Honey. Are you here?"

"Be right there."

He walked out of the kitchen with a vase of fresh roses. "I thought these would look good on the table."

"How sweet. They're lovely." She kissed his cheek. "Guess what?"

"What?"

"I filed the incorporation papers this morning, along with my request for nonprofit status, and my tax exemption. If it all goes through, my organization will be in full swing by my birthday."

"I'm impressed. You move fast."

"Not only that. I found a cute shop that'll make the plaques. The first four will be ready in two weeks, and at a good price, too."

"Four?"

"For Kate, Kim, Marge and myself."

"Your friends will be so proud. Have you talked to them lately?"

"Only Kim and Kate. I haven't been able to reach Marge. I hope she's okay."

"Why wouldn't she be?"

"I don't know. Of all of us, she seemed to be the one most unsettled. She's probably busy."

"You know, if this organization doesn't work out, I make enough to take care of both of us."

She hugged him. "I appreciate the offer, but I'm not marrying you to have someone to take care of me. I intend to carry my weight in this relationship."

He stammered, "I know. I didn't mean to imply you wouldn't make it. I just wanted you to know, I'd be there for you."

"That's all I need—your support and love. Thank you."

That evening, Denise asked, "Have you thought any more about where we'll live?"

"Why don't we rent out both houses and buy one together?"

She thought. "I like the idea of buying a house together, but I want to help buy it. The only way I could do that is to sell mine."

He stood. "I knew you'd say that. Hear me out. I prepared for this. You mentioned you wanted a prenuptial agreement to protect me. I don't see the need for it. I want everything I have to be yours, too. I know you won't rip me off or take advantage of me."

Denise frowned and started to speak, but he held up his hand.

"I'll make a deal with you. I'll give you a prenuptial agreement if you'll let me buy the house we live in. If you aren't going to stake any claim on me, then I'd like to provide my new bride with a home as a wedding present. Besides, it can be covered in the agreement if you want."

She hugged him. "You're so sweet."

He grinned. "Besides, if this doesn't work out, you'll have your home as a security blanket. If I get to keep what's mine, you should keep what's yours. What do you say?"

"Okay, as long as you sign a prenuptial agreement."

"I don't understand why it's so important to you, but if it makes you happy, I'll sign. We can always change things later."

"Thanks. It is important to me."

He kissed her and held her tightly. "Whenever you like, we can start house hunting."

"Let's start after my birthday. We'll have plenty of time to find something we both like and get things settled before the wedding."

"Speaking of that, have you given any thought to where and what kind of ceremony?"

Denise sighed, "I always wanted a church wedding, with an old, traditional ceremony. Nothing big, just friends and family."

"That's fine. What about the reception?"

"Heavens, I haven't gotten that far."

"How about a special sit-down dinner in the banquet room at Eugene's. They said they'd give me a deal on food and drinks. I think they'd be offended if we went elsewhere."

Denise laughed, "Wonderful idea."

Their discussion was interrupted by the telephone. Denise answered.

"Hello?"

"Denise, is that you?"

"Yes, Kate."

"In person?"

"What are you up to?"

"There are several reasons for this call. I wanted to know how the foundation is coming, and I have some disturbing news. Finally, have you spoken to Marge lately?"

"Which should I answer first? I have filed the paperwork for the foundation and it should be up and running soon. I haven't talked to Marge. I've left messages for her to call, but she hasn't. I even wrote to her."

"I've tried reaching her too. Her husband said he'd tell her to call back, but she hasn't. I hope she's all right."

Me too. Listen, we've set New Year's Eve for the wedding. You'll come, won't you?"

"Wouldn't miss it for anything."

"Things still going well for you?" Denise asked.

"Couldn't be better. Ronald and I are happy. I sold my share of the partnership, and it looks like my Liz Claiborne shop will open the end of September."

"Super, so what's the disturbing news?"

Kate took a deep breath. "Remember how I was going to solve the Julia mystery and everything?"

"Sure. Did you find out anything?"

"I'm still tracking down Julia, but I've discovered lots of other things."

"Like what?"

"For starters, remember Jan and the jet we were in?"

"Of course. How could I forget?"

"Did you pay attention to the time we dropped you off in Dallas?"

"No."

"I didn't either, but when we landed in New York, it was still light and my watch read two minutes after six."

"So?"

"So, we left Tahoe at three o'clock. I remember Marge saying her watch started and it was 3:02."

"I don't follow."

"The point is, it would've been six in New York when we left Tahoe. We made two stops before I got home, yet my watch read 6:02."

Denise laughed, "Come on, Kate. Our watches hadn't worked for three days. You can't expect it to be correct."

"Maybe so, but with the time difference and all that flying, it should've been dark when I landed."

"I don't know how to answer that. Maybe it's one of those inexplicable things like at the castle."

"Fine, but that's not the only strange thing."

"What else?"

"I checked with air traffic control to see who filed the flight plan and everything. You have to have one, you know. Well, there's no record of that plane coming to New York on Friday or Sunday. They said it never landed."

Denise was pensive. "That does sound odd, but maybe they lost the flight plan. It could happen with a private plane, don't you think?"

"No way. They record all transmissions between the tower and the planes. There's no record of our pilot requesting landing instructions. We checked with Dallas, Minot and Lake Tahoe, and they have no records, either."

"Maybe you didn't talk to the right people," Denise suggested.

"I see you aren't going to believe any of this. Okay, try this one. I wrote down the plane's tail numbers. It took some digging, but I discovered the plane was registered to Jan Longview from Lake Tahoe."

"Good. Now we know her name."

"It's not funny, Denise. Records show that plane was lost in a snowstorm in the Sierras two years ago. The plane and pilot were never found. We got the newspaper article from Tahoe, and the picture is of Jan, the woman who flew us."

"What?"

"They've been missing two years."

Denise was silent.

"Are you still there?"

"I think so. I don't know what to say. Have you talked to the others?"

"Just Kim. I hope Marge hasn't disappeared, too"

Denise was nervous. "This is frightening. Are you certain?"

"We've checked and double-checked. Ronald couldn't believe it either. I found Jan's husband and spoke to him on the phone. He's still in Tahoe. He was real upset with my call. I couldn't tell him I'd seen Jan, so I made up something about writing an article on missing aircraft. He said her aircraft disappeared one night. There was no distress signal or sign of trouble. They've never found any trace of her or the plane."

"There must be some explanation," Denise insisted.

"I'm sure there is, but I'll be damned if I know what it is. Julia's the only one who can answer that. There's more."

"More?"

"I tried to track down Hildy and her limousine. They don't exist either. Nevada has never issued that personalized license plate, and none of the limousine services in Tahoe have heard of Hildy or the castle."

"The limo could have been privately owned. We didn't know Hildy's last name."

"In light of the missing plane, I thought it odd we now have a

232

missing limo. Don't you?"

"Have you tried to reach Julia?"

Kate sighed, "I tried. There's no such number. According to the phone company, there never was an 800 number like the one we called. There's no record of the fax numbers I used. No one ever received my faxes. The prefix for that area doesn't even match the number we used. The post office doesn't even have a box with that number."

"This is scary."

"Want to hear more?"

"Not really."

"Too bad. Listen to this. When I spoke to Kim, she was upset. She shot four rolls of film, and all the negatives came out blank. She had her camera checked, and there was nothing wrong with it. Then, she took her partner back to Tahoe to show her the castle, and it was gone."

"Kate, she must've been confused about the location."

"Denise, we're talking about a mountain woman who marks her trail and never gets lost."

"It could happen...."

"I doubt it. You're going to hate this next part. Kim checked with the casino where we had dinner and saw the show. She thought maybe they'd have a record of the reservations or a credit card payment for our bill. Well, they told her k.d. lang has never performed in Tahoe."

Gooseflesh appeared all over Denise's body. "What do you think this means? We couldn't have been dreaming."

"Of course not. We knew this wasn't a normal conference, but this goes beyond abnormal. Julia is the key. I'm still working on her."

"What do you think we should do?"

233

"Kim and I think we should get together and go to Tahoe again. Are you willing?"

"Yes, but I'm frightened."

"No kidding. I'm petrified. But, we were safe when we were together before, so Kim and I decided we'd be safe as a group. We thought the weekend after Labor Day would be good. If we fly into San Francisco, Kim will pick us up."

"Would we go to Tahoe together?"

"Yeah. Kim said she'd drive us."

"Okay, count me in. What about Marge?"

"I'll keep trying. She needs to come, too."

"What if she disappeared?"

"If she did, she did it on her own. No one in their right mind would tangle with her."

"You're right. Please keep in touch."

"I will."

Denise hung up and walked slowly into the kitchen.

"Who was that?" he asked.

"Kate."

"What's the matter? You look worried."

Denise quickly related what she learned.

"Maybe it's not a good idea for you women to go back there. It might be dangerous."

Denise smiled, "Don't worry. It might be strange, but it's not dangerous. No matter who Julia is, she'd never let anything happen to us. Our personal guides will look after us, too."

"Perhaps, but be careful. I'd hate to lose you now."

"You won't. Besides, this is a good excuse for a reunion. We'll have had our birthday celebrations and have plenty to share."

CHAPTER THIRTY-TWO

The conference call between the four women brought them up-to-date on each other's lives, and Kate's investigation. They finalized plans for the September reunion.

Kim was so excited about her friends coming, she took off from school and was at the airport an hour early. Kate was scheduled to arrive at two, Denise at two forty-five, and Marge at three-thirty.

Kim paced the corridor near Gate 22, waiting for Kate's plane. She kept looking at the piece of paper containing everyone's flight number and arrival time. It seemed an eternity since they had been at Lake Tahoe.

Kate's declaration that she finally uncovered some mystifying information about Julia, had Kim excited. Kate had already learned more than they wanted to know. What else could she spring on them?

Kate was the first off the plane. Kim waved and dashed to greet her.

"What did you do, fly first class?" Kim asked.

"Of course. You ask?"

They hugged, blocking the path of others trying to deplane.

"I'm so glad to see you," Kim said.

"Me too. I've felt so alone and disjointed about this whole thing. It's wonderful to know you exist. Nothing else about that conference fits."

"So, what's the big news about Julia? I've been dying to know."

"And, I'm dying to tell you, but I want to share it when we're all together. I have to see your expressions. You won't believe it."

"Oh, I wish they were here now. I can't wait."

They both looked around as though they expected the others to magically appear.

"I guess wishing only works at the castle," Kate laughed.

They walked arm-in-arm down the stairs to the baggage claim.

"Let's get a cart," Kim suggested.

"Why? I only brought one bag."

"Fine, but there are two others coming. We can load everyone's and not have to carry anything. I brought quarters for the machine."

"Good idea. Who knows how many suitcases Marge will bring?"

"She's the last one to arrive," Kim stated.

"Figures. That way, she can make a grand entrance. Let's have a pool. Denise can join when she gets here. For five bucks, you get one guess on how many pieces of luggage Marge brings. Winner takes all."

"I'm in, but her purse doesn't count."

"Yes, it does. She uses a saddlebag for a purse and can stuff as much in it as I get in an overnight bag."

Kim agreed, "You're right. In that case, I'll say three."

"That was going to be my guess. Okay, I'll take two. Denise can have four."

"What if she only has one bag or as many as five?"

"If it's one bag, we give her the money and faint. If it's more than four, we send her back to Minot on the next flight."

As they waited for Kate's luggage, Kim asked, "Do you think Marge is okay? She seems lost."

Kate shook her head. "Marge has been lost for a long time. The castle thing only confused her more. For the first time in her life, she's alone and doesn't know how to deal with it yet. I'm not certain, but I think the booze has made things worse. Every time I talk to her, she's been drinking."

"She admitted it?"

"Well, she didn't say she had a problem with it, but she did say she should cut down. Once she told me Walter tried to get her to go to Alcoholics Anonymous, but she thought he was the one with the problem, not her."

When the bag arrived, they placed it on the cart. "People must think we're wimps pulling one small bag around on a cart," Kim said.

"Who cares? They don't want to say anything to two menopausal women. One's bad enough. Two will stomp the stuffing out of someone."

"How you doing with it?" Kim asked.

"Just bitchin', or is it bitchy? I seem to be full of the classic symptoms—hot flashes, PMS, insomnia, and vaginal dryness. How about you? Are you into it?"

Kim beamed. "I sure am. All I've had so far are the hot flashes. I had my first one on the way home from the castle."

"No kidding?"

"Seriously. I was so happy. I haven't had a period in two months, and I'm thrilled."

"Periods convinced me God wasn't a woman. She'd never have put up with such things. So, anything else?"

Kim thought. "Not that I've noticed. I do seem a little more emotional than usual."

"In what way?"

"You know, stupid things, like I cry at the McDonald's commercials. Linda says I'm testy over things that never used to bother me, but she admits it's nothing like what she went through."

"Are you taking hormone therapy?"

"Not yet. If I get really strange, I'll probably do it. They say there are a lot of benefits. How about you?"

"I haven't decided."

"They sure have helped Linda."

Some men bumped into Kate, glared and stomped off, without speaking.

"Hey, Bucko!" she called. "Better watch who you're running into. We haven't had our drugs yet. We're dangerous."

They were still laughing as they sank into seats to wait for Denise.

"How much longer after Denise arrives do we have to wait for Marge?"

"Forty-five minutes, if the plane's on time."

"Not bad."

They saw Denise's plane taxi to the terminal.

"Wanna bet she's not first?" Kate asked.

"Are you kidding? A safer bet would be that she's the last one off. She probably flew stand-by, because it's cheaper."

"She's too cheap to fly first class even with a rich boyfriend."

Kim choked. "That's not it. If the plane goes down, she wants everyone to know she was the last to give up."

They started laughing and laughed even harder as each person deplaned without it being Denise. They were almost falling on the floor by the time she finally came up the ramp. Tears were streaming down Kim's cheeks as she hugged her friend.

"What's so funny?" Denise asked.

Kate looked down the ramp. "Anyone else left on board?"

"The stewards and pilots."

Kate and Kim held their sides, laughing so hard, they could barely walk.

"What's so damn funny?"

"Denise," Kim gasped for air, "you had to be here to appreciate the joke. We were betting you'd be the last one off the plane."

"Couldn't you two find anything better to do while you waited?"

They walked with their arms around each other, moving in and out of groups of people so they wouldn't bump anyone. They refused to let go of each other.

"We've got another bet going," Kim said.

"It better be about Marge. What is it?"

"We each put up five bucks and guessed how many pieces of luggage she'll bring. Winner takes all."

Denise shook her head. "Does her purse count as one piece?"

"You bet."

Denise stopped and pulled out a five-dollar bill. "I'll guess four, unless someone has that number."

"It's yours," Kim smiled. "I've got three and Kate has two."

They sat and waited for Marge's plane. "Do you think she's okay?" Denise asked.

"We don't know," Kate confessed.

"She seemed so disoriented the last time I spoke with her. She has some big expectations on this trip."

"In what way?"

"She thinks she can go back to the lake and find all the answers to things in her life."

"I think we're going to come away with more questions," Kate sighed.

"That reminds me," Denise said. "You have information about Julia? What is it?"

"It's big and frightening. I'm saving it until we're all here."

"Come on. I hate waiting. Besides, Marge probably can't handle it."

Kim looked out the window. "You won't have to wait long. Here comes her plane."

A few minutes later, Marge sauntered off the plane as if she were the only one on it. She wore her best cowboy boots, and old pair of Levi's that were so tight they looked painted on, and a new flannel shirt, unbuttoned to reveal cleavage. Her saddlebag was thrown over one shoulder.

"That's one," Kim eyed the purse.

Marge saw them and shouted, "God, is it hot in here?"

"Hot flash!" Kate yelled back.

Marge ran to embrace them. "Hot flash, hell. I haven't started that shit yet. I could still have a child if I wanted."

"That would be considered cruelty to children," Denise said.

"The hard part would be finding someone to father the child," Kim teased.

"You guys...oops, I meant women...think you're so funny. Just because there's no man in my life right now doesn't mean I couldn't get one if I wanted."

"Yeah, yeah," Denise mumbled.

"It's great to see all of you again." She threw open her arms and started a group hug.

At the baggage claim area, Denise asked, "What kind of luggage are we looking for?"

"How many pieces?" Kate added, grinning.

"It's blue," Marge replied.

"All of them?" Kim continued.

"I only brought one," Marge was indignant. "It's not like I'm staying a week."

"One suitcase and your purse?" Denise questioned.

"Yeah. Why?"

The women began laughing as Kim dug into her pocket and handed fifteen dollars over the Kate, who waved it in the air.

"What'd you turkeys do, bet on how many bags I'd bring?" Marge asked.

They nodded.

"Kate guessed two," Kim said.

"I've only got one."

"We counted your purse as one."

Marge joined in the laughter as they loaded her suitcase on the cart and headed toward the parking lot.

CHAPTER THIRTY-THREE

After the luggage and women were packed in the car, Kim left the airport and took the freeway toward San Francisco.

As soon as they were settled, Marge said, "Okay, Kate. Spill the beans about Julia."

"Yes," Denise agreed. "We're dying to hear the news."

Kate turned in the passenger seat so she could eye them. "Here goes. Tracking her down wasn't easy. We had to...."

"Spare all the details," Marge insisted. "Cut to the core."

"I hope you're ready."

Kim laughed. "As if we could be ready to find out our weekend never happened, the people we met don't exist, and the plane you flew in disappeared two years ago. How much worse can it be?"

"I warned you. I found several Julia Worthingtons, but only one that could be ours. The rest were much too young. A Julia Worthington was born on July 31, 1895, at nine forty-five in the morning in San Francisco. Her parents were Frank and Bonita Worthington."

"Sounds like her. Where is she?" Marge asked.

Kate hesitated. "That poses a problem. This Julia Worthington was stillborn. She never took a breath."

"Then how do you know about her? They don't keep records on stillborns, do they?"

"I didn't think so, but I found a great-grandniece of hers, and she said Julia's parents requested a birth certificate be issued, because it would the only thing of hers they had. The niece also told me that no death certificate was ever issued. Back then, such things weren't important. Julia's parents always treated things as though Julia were still alive because there was no death certificate. She said their family has passed the story down for years that Julia is still alive and looking over all of them. Here's the sad part. Both her parents died less than a year later, apparently of broken hearts."

Marge snorted. "If you think I'll believe we spent the weekend with a woman who never lived, you're crazy. There's no way it could be that woman. This gets more ridiculous every time we discuss it. I don't know who you are, but at least you're real. We saw the same things."

Kim nodded, "I have to agree with Marge. This is too strange, Kate. Maybe we haven't found the right Julia. Birth records weren't kept that well one hundred years ago. We might never find her."

"Maybe so," Denise said, "but think about it. What are the odds of a girl being born at that time on that date in San Francisco named Julia Worthington? There couldn't be two of them."

"Do you know where the Masonic Cemetery is?" Kate asked.

"Sure," Kim answered.

"This particular Julia Worthington is buried there."

Silence descended. They drove in quietly, each trying to sort out her feelings. Kim turned off the freeway and drove down several side streets toward the cemetery. She turned at the Masonic Cemetery sign and stopped at the office.

"All right, Kate, go ask where her plot is," Kim directed.

"Come with me," Kate pleaded. "You'll have to follow their directions.

A few minutes later, the two women returned to the car.

"Don't tell us the grave mysteriously disappeared," Marge said.

Kim and Kate didn't answer. Kim drove past hundreds of grave sites. Finally, she stopped.

"It'll be over there," she pointed. "Is everyone coming?"

They climbed out of the car slowly and started searching. They found the small grave with the name Julia Worthington engraved on it. It was unkempt and looked as if it hadn't been cleaned off in years. Kate took a tissue from her purse and wiped off the marker.

Julia Worthington

July 31, 1895

May she rest in

God's eternal castle

"Does that really say castle?" Denise asked. "What a strange thing to put on a grave."

"That's what it says," Kim confirmed. "There's something else here, too."

She brushed the marble slab harder and they knelt to look. On the marker was a small etching of a castle. All four women grabbed the gold pendants they were wearing.

"My God!" Marge screamed. "It's exactly like the ones we're wearing."

"You're right," Kate whispered.

"Come on," Denise whined. "Don't all castles look like this?"

"No," Kim answered. "This one's different. I thought they were unique when Marge gave them to us. I've never seen one quite like it."

"This still doesn't prove anything," Marge was adamant.

"What were we trying to prove?" Denise questioned.

"I have no idea," Kate sighed. "All I wanted was some information on the woman who gave us such a terrific weekend. She did so much for us. I wanted something concrete we could hang onto. Instead, I've created uncertainty and confusion."

Kim was philosophical. "We have something concrete to hold onto—each other. It never would've happened without that weekend in Tahoe. We found inner strengths, new goals, created our own rite of passage, and have bonds with new friends that will last forever."

Denise interrupted, "Hell, we could have turned fifty and no one would've cared, not even us. We could've slipped away and become old, like other women before us. Our lives could've been disasters if we hadn't taken a good look at ourselves and made some changes."

Kate nodded. "You're right. It doesn't matter what physical trappings helped us gain our new perspectives. Maybe it's the process. It's something that comes from within. I wonder if other women who really seem together and happy after menopause went through something like this?"

"If they did, and figured it out like we have, I'm sure they'd never tell anyone," Denise noted.

"No wonder people think older women are crazy," Kim said. "Maybe we are, look what we went through."

Marge scowled, "It sounds pretty hunky-dory for you three, but what about me? I don't have new perspectives or inner peace? I had a party, that's all."

They started walking toward the car.

"What do you mean, you don't have inner peace?" Denise asked.

"My husband left me, my boyfriend's engaged to a friend of mine, and everyone keeps telling me I drink too much."

"Do you?"

"Maybe I was, but I haven't had anything since my party."

"That's a good start," Kim said.

"Maybe you should go to Alcoholics Anonymous," Denise suggested.

"I went once. They want you to admit alcohol is more powerful than you, and you have no control over it."

"What's wrong with that?"

"I'm a bigger person than that."

Kate smiled. "You have control over everything else in your life. Why not admit you might be human and there's one thing you can't control?"

"I never thought of it that way, but I don't feel I'm in control of anything."

"How's your business?" Kim asked.

"Great. I have more work than ever."

"Then you must be in control of that."

"Yeah, but I don't have a man in my life."

"Are you happier?" Kate continued.

"I guess so. My life is less complicated."

"Does anyone run your life?" Denise pursued.

"Okay, I see what you're getting at. Maybe I have been looking at it all wrong. I am happier now. I love being alone and with my dog, Lobo. I have more time to do the things I want to do."

"Maybe you don't need a man right now," Denise commented.

"Easy for you to say. Look at the size of that diamond you're wearing."

Denise pushed Marge gently. "Yeah, easy for me to say. While you were out screwing your brains out all those years, I wasn't getting any. It's my turn to make up for lost time."

"Oooh! Are you sleeping with Gene before you're married?" Marge quipped.

Denise blushed, "That's none of your damn business."

"Look at that smile," Kate teased.

"Not to change the subject," Denise said quickly, "but what are the plans for the weekend?"

Kim answered as she drove down the street to her house, "Linda will take care of dinner for us tonight, and...."

"She's cooking for all of us?" Kate asked.

"No, she's taking care of dinner. She's having it delivered."

They laughed as Kim parked the car.

"I thought we'd get up early and drive to Tahoe. I made reservations at a motel for tomorrow night. Other than that, it's up to us."

"I want to go back to the castle," Marge said.

"Why don't we start at the airport and retrace our route?" Denise offered.

"I want to have some fun and enjoy the reunion," Kate said. "It seems we already found what we came for. We have each other. We won't find anything else. Let's take in a show or something."

"Oh, poo," Marge joked. "I want something more than each other and inner peace."

"Come on, Marge. How many women our age have peace of mind and inner strength?" Kate pointed out. "You have to admit, being with us is better than anything else you could be doing right now."

Marge bowed her head, "You've got a point."

That night the women sat on the floor of Kim's living room for hours. Linda and Bailey went to bed while they shared stories about their rites of passage.

"How'd things go on your birthday, Kim?" Kate asked. "You only said you had a wonderful time, and your family was back together."

Kim was animated, "You wouldn't believe it. It was magnificent. Linda and I printed announcements saying these people had won an all-expense-paid vacation to Lake Shasta for a weekend on a houseboat. Everyone fell for it. A couple were sorry I hadn't won and felt guilty they wouldn't be here for my birthday. I told them to go ahead, we'd celebrate later. It was a scream to hear them rave about winning something."

"How many were there?" Marge asked.

"Sixteen, plus Linda, Bailey and me."

"Where did you put them?" Denise asked.

"We rented two houseboats. We were there early and had everything all ready when they arrived. You should've seen the expressions on their faces when they realized they'd been set up."

"How did your parents react?" Kate questioned.

"At first, Mom was angry she'd been duped. Dad loved it. He thought it was a stroke of genius. He convinced Mom to stay. Anna and John were there, too. Dad told her it was a good chance to patch things up without losing face."

"Did it work?"

"Like a charm. We mixed up the groups on the two houseboats. Mom was never sure who was gay and who wasn't."

"What a hoot!" Kate said.

"By the end of the weekend, Mom was telling everyone what to do and treating them like family. Oh, one other thing happened, too. Mom, Linda, and another friend of ours went on a five-mile swim. Mom challenged them."

"She's that good?" Denise queried.

"No. She thought it was five miles from the boat to the end of the cove and back. It might have been a quarter mile. Mom's no good with distances. Anyway, she got a cramp in her leg and the other two had to tow her back. She thinks they saved her life. They never told her the water was about five feet deep. Now, they're best of friends."

"She and Linda?" Kate was surprised.

Kim laughed, "It gets worse. It's sickening. She's trying to convince herself that Linda's really Japanese. When she calls, she spends more time talking to Linda."

"I'm so happy to hear things turned out for you," Denise beamed. "Maybe some of the magic of the castle wore off."

They finally grew tired and went to bed, but they shared a group hug before retiring. Each was anxious to revisit Lake Tahoe.

CHAPTER THIRTY-FOUR

Kim was the only one who seemed awake as the group left San Francisco. The others dozed. Ninety minutes later, they stopped at a restaurant in Davis for breakfast. As they ate, Marge said, "Linda could've come with us."

"Thanks, Marge. I didn't think you would mind, but we thought it would be more meaningful if the four of us made the trip. She and I come up often. I brought her up to show her where we stayed."

"You saw the castle?" Marge asked.

"No. We went to the spot, but it wasn't there. We hiked all over without finding a trace of anything."

"You must have been in the wrong place," Denise reasoned.

"I thought so, too, but I know we were at the right place."

"Didn't you do a lot of hiking when we were there?" Kate asked.

"Yes."

"Well..." Denise pursued.

"Well what? I know I was in the right place. I know where my tent was. Bailey knew it, too."

"And there was nothing?" Kate continued.

"There were no marks on the ground and none of my trail markers were there."

"What trail markers?" Denise wondered.

"I used stones, strings and marks on trees so we wouldn't get lost. They were all gone. I checked the whole side of the lake. We weren't on the other side, because the sun rose over the water."

"Was there anything familiar about the place?"

"Yes, I found the cove and beach where we went the last day. The tree with the three trunks is still there. I named it Three Tree Cove. Bailey recognized it. He barked and ran in the water."

"Then, let's go to the cove and backtrack," Marge insisted. "With all of us, we can find the castle. It didn't just disappear."

Kate was pensive, "Unless it never existed in the first place."

"Kate, we were there," Marge shouted.

"I've been there, Marge. The castle doesn't exist," Kim stated.

"Think about it," Kate proposed. "Maybe the castle only existed for that weekend, for one purpose."

"What are you saying?" Denise asked.

Kate was defensive, "How the hell do I know? I just think this whole thing is beyond anything we know."

"Like something from the *Twilight Zone?*" Denise asked.

"I don't believe in that stuff," Marge said.

"Perhaps that's why you're the only one still having problems," Kate answered.

"Oh, sure. Like if I believe in fairy tales, my life suddenly turns out fine?"

"I don't know," Kate grew impatient. "I think at some point here, we need to let go of trying to figure things out and just accept them."

Marge's face was red. "You're all going crazy. We'll find something. There has to be a logical explanation."

They finished breakfast and continued on Highway 50, winding through the mountains to the lake. Some trees were turning color, but it wasn't enough to herald the coming of fall.

"I'll bet this place is beautiful in winter," Denise observed.

"It is," Kim replied. "You should see it—mounds of deep white snow. It's gorgeous. It's peaceful and serene."

"I think it's like that without the snow," Kate added.

"Do you ski, Kim?" Denise asked.

"Cross country. It's a wonderful way to see the area."

"I probably couldn't do it."

"Sure you could. It's easy. Come out this winter. Linda and I will take you. Bring that man of yours, too."

Denise laughed, "I'll have to. He'll be my husband in a few months."

"I've got it," Marge announced. "Why don't you and Gene come here on your honeymoon? We could all meet and go skiing."

Kate rolled her eyes. "Just what they need—a bunch of fifty-year-old women skiing around the countryside looking for a castle."

"Changing the subject," Kim interrupted. "We're at the summit. In a few minutes, you'll see one of the world's most panoramic views."

The car started down the mountain.

"Get ready," Kim warned. "As soon as we round the next curve, well, there it is, see for yourselves."

Kim slowed and parked at one of the viewing points along the road. Everyone got out for a look.

"This is super," Kate stated. You can see forever from here. What a view."

"You can see the airport," Marge pointed out. "Look for the castle."

They returned to the car and made the rest of the trip down the mountain in silence. Kim drove to the airport.

"See? It's still here, just like I remember," Marge exclaimed.

Kate eyed Kim. "Do you remember the road we took from here?"

"Sure, it's easy."

As they drove down the road, Kate said, "This looks familiar."

"I specifically remember this part of the road," Kim stated. "I told Bailey it was strange that we were following a limousine, but there was no dust in our face."

The others turned back and looked.

"There's dust now," Marge said.

"Yes!" Denise shouted. "We turned left up here, and there was the castle."

They turned left. The clearing existed, but there was no sign of a castle.

"This is the place," Kim said.

"This is it," Marge agreed. "I feel it. Let's get out and see if we can find something."

Kim parked and everyone got out slowly.

"This clearing doesn't seem large enough for a castle," Denise said.

"How would we know?" Kate asked. "We never saw the whole thing."

"There's no sign of the garden conference room," Denise sighed.

Marge knelt down. "If there had been any kind of building here, there would be marks. There's no sign a building was ever here."

"This is creepy. What now?" Denise asked.

"Maybe Kim can take us to that cove," Marge suggested."

They easily found the trail and walked along quietly. Each was lost in thought, trying to assess her feelings about what was happening.

At the cove, the women threw themselves on the sandy beach, thrilled to see it was as they remembered. They stretched out as they had before and watched sunlight dance on rippling water.

"I wish Maddie were here," Marge mumbled. "She could clear things up. You know, I thought I saw her at my party, but I was so drunk, I wasn't able to get to her. I miss her. She was easy to talk to."

Marge stood and walked toward the water. Suddenly, she look up at the top of the bluff overlooking the cove. She blinked, rubbed her eyes, then waved. The others scrambled to their feet.

"Maddie!" Marge yelled. "Is that you?"

"Hi, everyone," Maddie said matter-of-factly.

"Are we glad to see you!" Marge exclaimed. "We thought we were going crazy. Where's the castle? Where's Julia?"

"Julia sent me. She said you needed help."

"You mean Julia exists?" Denise questioned. "Where is she? Did you bring our guides?"

Maddie held up her hands. "Ladies, Julia's not here, okay? You need to accept the fact that she doesn't exist in your world anymore. Stop trying to find her. It won't happen. I didn't bring your guides, because they are already with you, everyone except Marge. She's the only one who doesn't believe she has a personal guide on whom she can call throughout the rest of her life. I'm here to give her one final reminder. Julia said to let you know, once again, I'm here for you, even if you can't see me."

"I see you now."

"That's just so I can make a point."

"You are like guardian angels, aren't you?" Denise asked.

Maddie shrugged, "I'm probably not supposed to tell you this, but it's the only way Marge will figure it out. Think of us as your consciences."

"Then you don't exist," Marge stated.

"We do, within each of you."

"Is Julia the one we tracked down, the stillborn child?" Kate asked.

"It doesn't matter who she is. She said to tell you she thinks of you often and loves you very much. She's proud of how far you've come in such a short time, except for Marge."

"What's wrong with me?"

"You know the answer better than anyone. Ladies, it's time to let go. Get on with your lives and grow together."

She turned to Marge. "As for you, get your shit together. You know what to do. I'll be with you all the way."

"But...." Kim started.

"Sorry. That's all I can say." She walked away and waved as she went around the corner of the cove.

The women stared after her with their mouths open. After what seemed an eternity, Marge turned to her friends with tears in her eyes. She threw her arms around them, and they hugged her fiercely.

Marge smiled. "It's time to go."

EPILOGUE

Marge returned to North Dakota and resumed her contracting business, which flourished. She found the elusive inner peace, and grew in self-awareness and sensitivity.

She joined a local Alcoholics Anonymous group and stopped drinking. She sponsors many new members, conducts meetings and drinks imported water.

Marge occasionally saw Maddie, although no verbal contact was made. She knew Maddie heard her and silently guided her in her travels.

Marge also learned to develop meaningful relationships with men and women. She no longer jumped into bed with every exciting male she met. While she doesn't rule out the possibility of another marriage, she finds she can handle things on her own.

After divorcing Marge, Walter married a woman in Montana, and is happy. Greg married Ginny and helps with the catering business. They have two children. Marge is godmother to their daughter.

Marge has conducted several rites of passage for women in Minot, working closely with Denise to provide plaques for women turning fifty.

During the cold, harsh winters, Marge travels. She has taken up golf and has played on courses in Hawaii, the Bahamas, and Arizona.

Dallas is a frequent stop for Marge, where she helps Denise with her foundation. They have both traveled to New York to purchase fancy clothes at Kate's boutique. No one knows where or when she wears the clothes.

Marge was even seen in a gay bar in San Francisco, though she is always quick to point out she's not gay, merely enlightened. Some have said that Marge, for all her lack of understanding about other people's lifestyles, has occasionally worn out her welcome in Kim's home.

Kim's parents met Marge and were totally mystified by her behavior. They are thankful Kim is with Linda.

Kate and Ronald are happy. Kate has opened two more Liz Claiborne stores. She stopped to visit Marge once on her way to Liz' Montana ranch. Kate won the trip after having a high volume of business one year.

Visiting Marge was something Kate was glad she did once. Marge dressed her in Levi's, flannel shirts, and cowboy boots. Against her better judgment, Kate went for a horseback ride in the country with Marge. She didn't speak to her friend for several days, until she was able to sit comfortably again.

Ronald started his own law firm, specializing in civil rights cases. He chaired one of the largest New York chapters of the National Association for the Advancement of Colored People.

Kate says she talks with Kathy regularly, and is certain she has seen her at times. One of the things she is most proud of, besides her plaque from Denise, is the copy of the birth certificate she managed to obtain for Julia Worthington, born July 31, 1895. It hangs in her office.

Kim continues to build strong ties with her family, and was instrumental in forming a group that helps teenage Japanese lesbians in the Bay Area. Her parents have been supportive, and one year, marched in the Gay Pride parade.

Linda has spent a lot of time with Kim's mother, and has learned to cook Japanese food. Kim's mom said Linda would make an excellent cook if she'd stop using Tabasco sauce.

Kim and Linda invited the family for Christmas one year. Everyone stayed for three days, sleeping on the floor in sleeping bags, because no one would stay in a hotel and miss the fun. Kim's parents slept in her room, while she and Linda slept on borrowed cots. Linda was dubbed an honorary Japanese, and Kim's father once sent Linda a birthday card addressed to Linda Yamakara.

Kim admitted she never saw Karen again, but feels her presence.

Denise and Gene had a lovely wedding. Kim, Kate, and Marge attended and threw flowers. Gene has three restaurants, but turns the operation of them over to others so he and Denise can travel. They have been around the world, but their most enjoyable trips are to New York, San Francisco and North Dakota.

After being warned about Kate's horseback ride, Denise refused to get on a horse when they visited Marge. Gene humored her, however, and then complained for a month that his butt would never be the same.

Denise continued to try losing weight. Gene would praise her when she lost five pounds and pretended not to notice when she gained it back. Denise's parents moved into her old house.

The POWER foundation thrived. Denise was responsible for helping hundreds of women through their rite of passage. Danielle was listed as a member of the board of directors in an advisory capacity. Denise felt they were inseparable.

Reaching the foundation isn't easy. There is no listed address, telephone or fax number. Denise claims one can reach the foundation through the Rites of Passage Castle in Lake Tahoe, or by looking into one's heart and soul. And, she claims, anyone can reach the foundation through her personal guide.

For Kate, Denise, Marge and Kim, there is no doubt that the castle, Julia and their guides exist, even if they no longer exist in the same form in which they first met.

The idea of celebrating this stage of womanhood didn't start with Julia Worthington, and it wasn't brought to light by a gold-embossed, slightly raised and beautifully scripted invitation to a castle

Women throughout the world have been discovering their potential for years. Many are expressing a new freedom. For every woman who struggles with menopause, turning fifty, harassment, or abuse, there's a personal guide to help her break out of her mold. Women must keep an open mind and remember that their rite of passage is only what they make of it.

POSTSCRIPT

This author went through her own rite of passage (yes, I'm more than fifty years old). It took eight days and there were many memoriable experiences. It would take another book to enumerate them. For all those fantastic people who shared my rite of passage and were the inspiration for this book, I thank you.